Happily Ever Maybe

Also From Carrie Ann Ryan

The Montgomery Ink Legacy Series:
Book 1: Bittersweet Promises
Book 2: At First Meet
Book 2.5: Happily Ever Never
Book 3: Longtime Crush
Book 4: Best Friend Temptation
Book 4.5: Happily Ever Maybe
Book 5: Last First Kiss
Book 6: His Second Chance
Book 7: One Night with You

The Wilder Brothers Series:
Book 1: One Way Back to Me
Book 2: Always the One for Me
Book 3: The Path to You
Book 4: Coming Home for Us
Book 5: Stay Here With Me
Book 6: Finding the Road to Us
Book 7: Moments for You
Book 8: A Wilder Wedding
Book 9: Forever For Us

The First Time Series:
Book 1: Good Time Boyfriend
Book 2: Last Minute Fiancé
Book 3: Second Chance Husband

The Aspen Pack Series:
Book 1: Etched in Honor
Book 2: Hunted in Darkness
Book 3: Mated in Chaos
Book 4: Harbored in Silence
Book 5: Marked in Flames

The Montgomery Ink: Fort Collins Series:
Book 1: Inked Persuasion

Book 2: Inked Obsession
Book 3: Inked Devotion
Book 3.5: Nothing But Ink
Book 4: Inked Craving
Book 5: Inked Temptation

The Montgomery Ink: Boulder Series:
Book 1: Wrapped in Ink
Book 2: Sated in Ink
Book 3: Moments in Ink
Book 4: Seduced in Ink
Book 4.5: Captured in Ink
Book 4.7: Inked Fantasy
Book 4.8: A Very Montgomery Christmas

Montgomery Ink: Colorado Springs
Book 1: Fallen Ink
Book 2: Restless Ink
Book 2.5: Ashes to Ink
Book 3: Jagged Ink
Book 3.5: Ink by Numbers

Montgomery Ink Denver:
Book 0.5: Ink Inspired
Book 0.6: Ink Reunited
Book 1: Delicate Ink
Book 1.5: Forever Ink
Book 2: Tempting Boundaries
Book 3: Harder than Words
Book 3.5: Finally Found You
Book 4: Written in Ink
Book 4.5: Hidden Ink
Book 5: Ink Enduring
Book 6: Ink Exposed
Book 6.5: Adoring Ink
Book 6.6 Love, Honor, and Ink
Book 7: Inked Expressions
Book 7.3: Dropout
Book 7.5: Executive Ink
Book 8: Inked Memories

Book 8.5: Inked Nights
Book 8.7: Second Chance Ink

The On My Own Series:
Book 0.5: My First Glance
Book 1: My One Night
Book 2: My Rebound
Book 3: My Next Play
Book 4: My Bad Decisions

The Promise Me Series:
Book 1: Forever Only Once
Book 2: From That Moment
Book 3: Far From Destined
Book 4: From Our First

The Less Than Series:
Book 1: Breathless With Her
Book 2: Reckless With You
Book 3: Shameless With Him

The Fractured Connections Series:
Book 1: Breaking Without You
Book 2: Shouldn't Have You
Book 3: Falling With You
Book 4: Taken With You

The Whiskey and Lies Series:
Book 1: Whiskey Secrets
Book 2: Whiskey Reveals
Book 3: Whiskey Undone

The Gallagher Brothers Series:
Book 1: Love Restored
Book 2: Passion Restored
Book 3: Hope Restored

The Ravenwood Coven Series:
Book 1: Dawn Unearthed
Book 2: Dusk Unveiled

Book 3: Evernight Unleashed

The Talon Pack:
Book 1: Tattered Loyalties
Book 2: An Alpha's Choice
Book 3: Mated in Mist
Book 4: Wolf Betrayed
Book 5: Fractured Silence
Book 6: Destiny Disgraced
Book 7: Eternal Mourning
Book 8: Strength Enduring
Book 9: Forever Broken
Book 10: Mated in Darkness
Book 11: Fated in Winter

Redwood Pack Series:
Book 1: An Alpha's Path
Book 2: A Taste for a Mate
Book 3: Trinity Bound
Book 3.5: A Night Away
Book 4: Enforcer's Redemption
Book 4.5: Blurred Expectations
Book 4.7: Forgiveness
Book 5: Shattered Emotions
Book 6: Hidden Destiny
Book 6.5: A Beta's Haven
Book 7: Fighting Fate
Book 7.5: Loving the Omega
Book 7.7: The Hunted Heart
Book 8: Wicked Wolf

The Elements of Five Series:
Book 1: From Breath and Ruin
Book 2: From Flame and Ash
Book 3: From Spirit and Binding
Book 4: From Shadow and Silence

Dante's Circle Series:
Book 1: Dust of My Wings
Book 2: Her Warriors' Three Wishes

Book 3: An Unlucky Moon
Book 3.5: His Choice
Book 4: Tangled Innocence
Book 5: Fierce Enchantment
Book 6: An Immortal's Song
Book 7: Prowled Darkness
Book 8: Dante's Circle Reborn

Holiday, Montana Series:
Book 1: Charmed Spirits
Book 2: Santa's Executive
Book 3: Finding Abigail
Book 4: Her Lucky Love
Book 5: Dreams of Ivory

The Branded Pack Series:
(Written with Alexandra Ivy)
Book 1: Stolen and Forgiven
Book 2: Abandoned and Unseen
Book 3: Buried and Shadowed

Happily Ever Maybe
A Montgomery Ink Legacy Novella
By Carrie Ann Ryan

1001 DARK NIGHTS
PRESS

Happily Ever Maybe
A Montgomery Ink Legacy Novella
By Carrie Ann Ryan

1001 Dark Nights

Copyright 2024 Carrie Ann Ryan
ISBN: 979-8-88542-056-3

Foreword: Copyright 2014 M. J. Rose

Published by 1001 Dark Nights Press, an imprint of Evil Eye Concepts, Incorporated

All rights reserved. No part of this book may be reproduced, scanned, or distributed in any printed or electronic form without permission. Please do not participate in or encourage piracy of copyrighted materials in violation of the author's rights.

This is a work of fiction. Names, places, characters and incidents are the product of the author's imagination and are fictitious. Any resemblance to actual persons, living or dead, events or establishments is solely coincidental.

Acknowledgments from the Author

I need to thank Dylan Allen for getting me through this book. Writing our stories at the same time while realizing we need to write completely different stories really made me work harder and bring out the best romance for Jennifer and Gus!

Thank you to my Team Carrie Ann for making sure I get things done and for dealing with my spreadsheets of spreadsheets. I seriously couldn't be here without you!

Oh! And thank you to Liz, Jillian, and MJ. Thank you for trusting me and giving me a chance to write a romance I wouldn't get a chance to write!

And thank you always to my readers. You've been with me for over twelve years now and I cannot believe it. Thank you for making this job amazing! And here is to the next romance that makes me cry and swoon!

One Thousand and One Dark Nights

Once upon a time, in the future…

I was a student fascinated with stories and learning. I studied philosophy, poetry, history, the occult, and the art and science of love and magic. I had a vast library at my father's home and collected thousands of volumes of fantastic tales.

I learned all about ancient races and bygone times. About myths and legends and dreams of all people through the millennium. And the more I read the stronger my imagination grew until I discovered that I was able to travel into the stories… to actually become part of them.

I wish I could say that I listened to my teacher and respected my gift, as I ought to have. If I had, I would not be telling you this tale now. But I was foolhardy and confused, showing off with bravery.

One afternoon, curious about the myth of the Arabian Nights, I traveled back to ancient Persia to see for myself if it was true that every day Shahryar (Persian: شهریار, "king") married a new virgin, and then sent yesterday's wife to be beheaded. It was written and I had read that by the time he met Scheherazade, the vizier's daughter, he'd killed one thousand women.

Something went wrong with my efforts. I arrived in the midst of the story and somehow exchanged places with Scheherazade — a phenomena that had never occurred before and that still to this day, I cannot explain.

Now I am trapped in that ancient past. I have taken on Scheherazade's life and the only way I can protect myself and stay alive is to do what she did to protect herself and stay alive.

Every night the King calls for me and listens as I spin tales. And when the evening ends and dawn breaks, I stop at a point that leaves him breathless and yearning for more. And so the King spares my life for one more day, so that he might hear the rest of my dark tale.

As soon as I finish a story... I begin a new one... like the one that you, dear reader, have before you now.

Chapter 1

Gus

Distractions killed. At least in my line of business.

I needed to keep the bestselling author turned screenwriter turned Oscar-winner safe. He'd received a few death threats in the past thanks to his current work, and my job was to keep him protected. It wasn't any different than what I usually did. Keeping my client safe.

The man was currently on stage with a reporter from a major publication doing an interview in front of thirty-five hundred of their closest friends. I was off to the side, hands loose in front of me, looking as casual as possible as I kept scanning the room.

In addition to the death threats in the past two months, he'd also had some sexual innuendos and stalkerish behavior when it came to behind-closed-door activities.

I never understood the need to make up a relationship that had no chance of being real, yet these fans put their whole personalities into it. They sent him flowers, anniversary cards, and gifts just to remind him they existed and, in their minds, the two of them were in a relationship. It was downright terrifying, and while they weren't allowed on the premises, that didn't mean they couldn't find a way in.

The company I worked for had done background checks on the staff and other people here, but even though certain individuals were blacklisted from getting tickets, there were still ways to get through. And that's why I was here. Well, that's why the team was here.

I liked working for Montgomery Security. The crew I worked for was nearly all from the same family, or about to be related with an upcoming wedding. They were smart, diligent, and knew how to use their team.

I was damn good at being a bodyguard. I could usually sense a threat before it became a dangerous situation. In my last job, I stopped a young woman from throwing herself on the stage, screaming that she wanted to be with my client until the end of days. There hadn't been a scene. We had walked off calmly, and things were fine.

But for some reason, I was edgy now.

No, that was a lie. It wasn't just *some* reason. I knew exactly what it was.

And it wasn't Daisy and Kane, my fellow team members today. No, it was the other one.

Her.

I didn't want to think about her, but I wasn't sure I could stop. I needed to, however. My job demanded it.

I was a bodyguard and an installer. I not only protected my clients and charges, I also installed security equipment for businesses and homes. While my bosses laid out the security profiles and programs for large corporations and small residences—and also worked with cybersecurity—I did the installs when I wasn't on bodyguard duty. I enjoyed both aspects of my job and was talented at it.

Yet it didn't feel like that.

Not with her.

It was always hard to think about anything when it came to Jennifer. My coworker and my nemesis. Not that she knew she was my nemesis. No, that was all on me.

Those blue-gray eyes of hers were piercing and saw everything. At least when it came to the job. She could scent an incoming threat as quickly as I could, and that was saying something. I might be cocky as fuck when it came to my job, but it was for a reason.

And Jennifer was sometimes even better.

Her dark brown hair was pulled into a tight bun away from her face. I liked it when her hair was down, though, since it fell in soft waves past her shoulders. She pulled it back in a ponytail or a braid when she was working out, but when she was on duty, like today, it was in a bun, so nobody could use it against her in a fight.

I always kept my hair decently short, but my beard was getting longer. I'd probably have to trim it soon. I wasn't trying to blend in like I had with my old job when everybody had long beards, and I was undercover. Now, I needed to trim it a bit so nobody could pull it in a fight.

But Jennifer? She'd thought about all of that already. Hence the bun.

She was slim with a narrow waist and average height—though not much about her was *average*. But that delicate frame was all muscle. She could bench press more than a few of the guys on the team and kick any of our asses on any given day. Hell, she'd pinned me to the ground once, and I nearly swallowed my tongue. And then I'd had to hide my erection from her. Like I did most days. Because Jennifer was a distraction.

My distraction.

I pulled my gaze from her and wondered how she couldn't feel my eyes on her. I would think it would be piercing, as if she was the only thing that mattered. I could practically sense the heat of my gaze. Yet she couldn't feel me? That should worry me, or maybe I was just losing my damn mind because all I wanted was her. And that was a problem. Because we worked together.

I held back a snort at that. No, that wasn't the problem. Two of my bosses were getting married—not only to each other but also to the barista next door.

That made me smile because it was about damn time the three of them got together.

I had always thought Noah and Ford, while best friends, were better suited as something more. But it wasn't until Greer showed up that I realized what had been missing.

When it came to interdepartmental relationships, I didn't really care. It was fine as long as everyone kept their shit together and didn't let it interfere with work. Ford and Noah didn't. They loved each other, fought with each other, fought *for* each other, and kept the ship running.

Noah's cousins—Daisy, Kane, and Kingston—were also our bosses.

We had a few other part-time and contract workers who helped with installations and when we needed larger teams, but they liked being contractors because they could work for a few people and control their schedules. Jennifer and I were the only two full-time employees who weren't at the head of the company. It might seem awkward for some to be working with the Montgomerys so closely like that, but it worked for us. We got paid well, had decent benefits, and my dumbass could be near Jennifer more often.

I pulled my gaze from her and looked back at the crowd. Something tingled, and it wasn't just that I couldn't keep my eyes off Jennifer. While that was a problem, it wasn't the only one.

My client laughed at something on stage, and so did the crowd, but I was missing someone. I'd seen something, missed *something*.

"You okay, Gus?" Jennifer asked, her voice low, slightly smoky in a way that only happened when she was on duty.

I wondered what it would sound like in bed. But just because we had chemistry and constantly flirted with each other didn't mean I was allowed to think about that.

There were rules and guidelines about that. That had to be some form of sexual harassment. There was something fucking wrong with me.

"Just getting an itch," I whispered into the receiver.

Of course, that itch only partially had to do with something I sensed in the crowd. But I wouldn't put that out into the universe.

"I have a disturbance in section four. I'm going to check it out." Daisy's voice was low as she moved forward, and I was grateful that she was on it. She was still recovering from the incident that'd nearly killed her and scared all of us. But she was fine now, or so she said. I knew that Kane would be keeping an eye on her. They were cousins, just like most of our workforce, and he would ensure she was good. They were partners here, while Jennifer was mine.

"Are you sure everything is good?" she asked, her voice still low.

"Yeah. We're good."

She moved closer to me so we weren't talking on the mics. "I don't see anything on my end. What about you?"

I could feel her heat, just like always. I was in fucking trouble. But it was *my* problem. We had been flirting off and on since we met. We enjoyed it, the chemistry and heat between us. And we ignored it. We checked each other out and joked about going out, but we never did anything. Everybody gave us shit about it, too. It didn't matter because we all made it work, and we never let it get in the way.

And yet, it felt like something was off. Like something was different about this. Or maybe that was just me. Perhaps she didn't want anything more than joking, and that was why I was so distracted.

"False alarm," Daisy said over the earpiece, and I nodded, though she couldn't see me.

"Understood," Jennifer and I said at the same time as we kept our eyes on the audience.

"What's wrong?" Jennifer asked softly, and I turned to her.

"Nothing's wrong. I'm just trying to focus."

"I know. Same here. Did you see something? You seem off."

I was off because of her, but it wasn't as if I was going to tell her that.

We both turned back to the audience, though I wanted to say something. Only it seemed I had been distracted, after all.

"Dylan! I love you. Won't you think of our future children?"

We were off in an instant, moving before the woman even finished her statement. I went toward our client, Dylan, and Jennifer was on the woman as she screamed about her long-lost love as the crowd started screaming and yelling.

She threw a water bottle—just a water bottle—and it splashed all over the podium. I didn't know what was in it, if it was acid, something combustible, or worse, but I got the client away, all the while knowing I'd fucked up.

I had once again been distracted by Jennifer, talking to her when I should have been paying attention. When I *saw* the glint in that woman's eyes and ignored it because I wanted to look at a person I shouldn't.

Everything moved fast after that. Kane spoke over the intercom, telling the people to remain calm as we escorted the woman out. The authorities would be called, and we would deal, but I had fucked up.

"Let me go back out, it's fine. It's happened before." Dylan ran his hands through his hair and looked at me. "Don't kick yourself about this. It's not your fault."

I raised a brow. "I'm going to have to disagree, sir. But we'll handle it."

"It's fine. Nobody was hurt. I just hope she's okay."

The man was so damn nice. Nicer than I would've been. Then again, I was on the other side of the dividing line. The guy who was supposed to protect him. And I'd nearly failed.

"Can you take my spot?" I asked Kane, who gave me a look but nodded. I went to Daisy's side to take the back of the building. Dylan would finish the interview. And then we could regroup.

I would have to pretend that I hadn't just fucked up.

Still, I couldn't help but think about the one woman I shouldn't. My partner. Not my lover.

* * * *

When we got back, we were all exhausted, and Kane was on the phone with Ford. "Got it. Yeah, we'll meet you tomorrow." He hung up and looked at us. "It's late. We'll go over everything later. But from what we can tell, there wasn't anything we could have done differently. The auditorium allows water bottles. And according to the authorities, it was just water. It happens. We'll go through training again to make sure it doesn't happen again. Don't kick yourself. We got it done."

I nodded but didn't say anything. Jennifer frowned at my side. Daisy started limping to the door, and Kane cursed under his breath. "I'm going to make sure she gets home."

I sighed and nodded at him. "We'll close up."

"Yeah, just make sure she didn't overdo it today," Jennifer added.

And with that, it was just me and Jennifer alone in the office.

The one place I didn't want to be.

"So, what the hell was that?" Jennifer snapped.

I whirled on her. "What the hell was what?"

"That expression. Why are you glaring at me? It's not our fault. Yes, we missed the woman rushing the stage, but we got her before she could do any real damage. It could have been worse, but we got her. The client is safe, everybody who needed to have fun at the event did, and they also have a story to tell."

"Yeah? And if I wasn't fucking distracted by you, then maybe I would've caught it earlier." I hadn't meant to say that, and I had a feeling I should have kept my mouth shut.

Her eyes narrowed, her chest rising and falling in a rapid rhythm that drew my gaze before I looked back up to her eyes. "Excuse me? You're blaming me for this?"

I rubbed my hand over my face, knowing there was no way back from this particular conversation. I should have let it go. But I was a masochist with my emotions and didn't care. "No. I don't know. Hell, Jennifer, you're *always* a fucking distraction."

"Are you calling me unprofessional?"

"Of course, not. I'm calling you a *distraction*."

She sighed, meeting my gaze. "Explain. Tell me what the hell you're talking about because there's no way what happened is my fault."

"You know what you did. What you always do." I cursed. "That's not what I meant."

"What do you mean?"

"I can't keep my eyes off you, Jennifer. You know that. You know we flirt and joke around. Apparently, my dick couldn't get in line because all I could do was think about you. Want to be near you. And I missed the woman. So yes, it's your fault. Just as it's mine."

"Fuck you."

"That's the problem. I'm not."

She snorted. "If you wanted me, you could have had me when we first met. You're the one who walked away."

I staggered back, shocked. "What?"

"We went out the first night we met. I flirted hard, and you backed down."

I shook my head, not quite believing her. "I flirted right back. But I wasn't about to get in your pants the first day we met when we had to work together."

"You didn't want me. And now you're pretending you do and saying I'm the reason you fucked up? Which you *didn't*, by the way. Neither of us did. It happened; we fixed it. But it's not our fault. And it's damn sure not my fault that, apparently, you can't keep your eyes off me."

"I can't keep my eyes off you because you're the most beautiful woman I've ever met. You're hilarious, brilliant, and good at what you do. Plus, you're fucking sexy. That's why I can't keep my eyes off you."

"So somehow things I can't change are why you're pissed off at me?"

I threw up my hands. "I don't fucking know. I want you. And that's a problem."

She was silent for a few moments before seeming to come to a decision. "Then have me. Get it out of your system. And maybe I'll get it out of mine."

I must have fallen asleep and was in the middle of a damn wet dream, because there was no way I had heard what I thought I did. "What?"

"Do something about it. Because you're as much of a distraction for me."

I blinked at her, wondering what was going on. So, I figured…why not? Why *not* make this mistake?

I grabbed her shoulders and crushed my mouth to hers, hoping to hell we weren't making things worse.

Chapter 2

Jennifer

He tasted like coffee and Gus. I hadn't realized I craved this. No, that was a lie. Of course, I knew I wanted him. It was an issue. Perhaps not the problem he thought it was, but that was on him.

When he tugged on my hair, tipping my head back to deepen the kiss, I moaned, my fingernails digging into his hips. As he pulled away, panting, I licked my lips and looked up at him.

"Okay, then." I did my best to sound nonchalant, like I wasn't all worked up. But I was.

I was strong, smart, and could handle myself in any situation. I was in a job where many men outside my core group thought I was ill-equipped just because I had ovaries instead of a dick. Yet I could outclass them all. I knew how to get shit done. I knew how to stand on my own two feet.

But with Gus's hands on me, roaming over my body, touching, squeezing, tasting, it was hard for me to remember my name, let alone what I was supposed to be doing in the situation. Oh, yes, I should be taking control. Telling him to get over his fucking self and not blame me for his mistakes.

And yet…it wasn't there. All the words I needed were gone. Poof. I didn't care. I wanted more. Needed more.

"Jen," he whispered against me, nibbling my jawline.

I kept touching him but didn't respond.

"Do you really think this will solve anything?" he growled against my lips, even as he tugged my shirt up so he could touch skin. His fingers were rough and calloused, and it nearly sent me over the edge.

That was new and interesting—the idea of coming from merely a touch of skin against skin.

What was it about this man?

"Who's saying we want to solve anything?" I asked, sounding far more together than I felt.

He looked at me then. I stared into those eyes that did something to me and told myself it was fine. The thought of his beard against my skin and his calloused fingers against my flesh was enough. Only a taste for now so I could get over it. Get over *him*.

I knew it was a lie even as I thought it.

"Then we don't solve anything. We scratch the itch."

My lips twitched. "We both know I suck at relationships."

He laughed then, and it didn't quiet the intensity inside. If anything, it made it burn hotter. We knew each other. In the past year, we had risked our lives for each other, trusted each other with everything but the deepest parts of ourselves, the quietest parts. So, perhaps it made sense that him understanding me like that would turn me on even more.

"You know I'm not good at them either."

"Then we do our best not to be good at them together. Just for now. I'm *not* your distraction," I said again, annoyed by the hurt in my tone. Neither of us had done anything wrong. Things happened, and we adjusted; everyone was safe. But if Gus thought he had done something and was lashing out because of it? I wasn't going to be his punching bag.

"You're sure as hell a distraction right now," he mumbled against me. In answer, I crushed my mouth to his. I was tired of this conversation. I just wanted to do the thing I'd been imagining since I met him—taste him.

He slid his hands up my shirt, and I pulled back, arms over my head as he tugged it off.

I did the same to him, and then his fingers were suddenly on my bra, the tan fabric falling to the floor. I groaned when his hands moved to my chest, his thumb and forefinger playing with my nipple. I didn't have large breasts; they barely filled his palms, but they were sensitive.

When he kept rolling them, I groaned and rocked into him. I could feel his erection against my stomach. He was long, thick—a fucking steel pipe. And soon, it would be *mine*.

I grinned against his lips before his mouth went to my nipple, sucking on the bud. He bit down gently, and the sensation warmed me from the inside. I pressed my thighs together, my clit throbbing with each heartbeat.

"So fucking beautiful," he whispered before moving me to my desk. We were in the middle of the office. Anyone with a key could walk in at any moment. And we knew every single person who had a key.

But I didn't care.

Instead, I put my hands on the desk and lifted myself up. When I put my butt on the surface, he grinned and lowered to his knees.

There was nothing more beautiful than a strong man with a muscled back kneeling between your legs.

It was a masterpiece. A fucking work of art.

When he undid my boots, I spread my legs for him, helping him when he went to my zipper.

"I need to taste you."

"Then get on it, big boy," I teased.

He grinned and smacked a kiss to my lips before pulling at my pants. I moved, feeling slightly vulnerable when he pulled my panties down. He was still partially dressed, his pants and boots on, and here I was, naked on my desk, my computer against my back.

He shifted me so there was nothing behind me, just a few files that weren't important.

And then he was on his knees again, his hands on my inner thighs.

He looked up at me, those eyes of his seeing far too much before he leaned down and pressed a soft kiss right above my knee.

I shivered, and my legs nearly clamped around his head.

He must have noticed the movement because he grinned before kissing my other thigh and trailing more toward my center. His beard was soft, which had surprised me during our kiss. He must use beard oil for it. It wasn't rough and dirty. I liked some things rough and dirty but not facial hair.

I needed him. And that should scare me because he was my friend. But this was just for today. Only for this moment. We were getting it out of our systems. I was fine with that.

And then his mouth was on my cunt, and I was swallowing hard, head thrown back as he licked and sucked at me.

"You're so fucking sweet. Like honey on my tongue."

I wasn't typically a fan of guys talking during sex. Usually, they just grunted and mumbled my name in an unintelligible way that said they weren't really into it, just getting off. But for some reason, I *wanted* Gus to talk. I needed him to tell me what I tasted like, what he desired.

As if he could read my damn mind, he did.

"You're going to come on my face, on my tongue, and then you're going to lay back so I can fill you with my cock. Are you ready for that, Jen?"

I licked my lips and slid one hand up to my breast, cupping myself. I pinched my nipple, meeting his gaze. "You talk a lot for a guy not getting me off."

He grinned as if it were a challenge—which it damn well was—before returning to eating me out, slowly delving his tongue between my folds. He didn't meet my gaze. Instead, he watched my wet pussy, enough that I should feel embarrassed, but I couldn't. All I could do was want him, crave him.

He lapped me up, his tongue twisting around my clit. When he speared me with two fingers, I wasn't prepared. I gasped, nearly falling off the desk. But he kept me steady, one hand on my thigh and the other fucking me, even as he continued to taste and lick.

It was too much. I put both hands on the desk, keeping myself steady so I wouldn't fall. And then I was coming, nearly ricocheting off the desk and onto his face as I trembled, my clit throbbing, my pussy clenching. But he continued to eat, kept savoring.

"That's my girl," he mumbled against me before kissing my pussy, then my thighs again. Before I could blink, he was licking and sucking up my body, paying particular attention to my nipples. Then his mouth was on mine, his hand on the back of my head, in control. And I let him. For this moment, I let him.

"Jen," he whispered.

"Oh, dear God. I knew you could do something better with that mouth than just drone on and on about reports." I winked as I said it, needing to settle into this moment.

He rolled his eyes before kissing me hard and gripping my wrist. "Now, be a good girl and suck my dick."

I should be offended, but I really wanted to see it. I didn't usually like them. They were ugly and awkward, but I really wanted to see his. So, I undid his pants, and we both worked them down over his very luscious ass. I swallowed hard.

He was thick, long, and the ring at the end was something I wasn't quite expecting.

"Look at you with the jewelry. Full of surprises." I licked my lips even as I gripped him in one hand, my thumb rubbing the jewelry at the tip.

"Well, your hand is like a fucking vise. If you're not careful, I'm going to come over those pretty tits and not in that pussy."

"I'm sorry. Is that a complaint?" I squeezed.

His eyes closed, and he gripped my wrist, keeping me steady. "I want to feel your pussy around me."

"We can make that happen. But the piercing?" I asked again.

He shrugged, the movement making my hand slide up and down his cock. We both groaned at that, and I kept working him slowly. I didn't want this to end, even though I knew it needed to. "We're friends with a bunch of tattoo artists and piercers. Of course, I have the ink and piercings."

I looked over his body, at the tattoos covering his chest and hips. I knew he had more on his back. After all, we worked out together, and I had seen him shirtless countless times. But I had never seen him like this.

Damn the man. "Well, I like it."

"I'm surprised you're not more pierced."

I shimmied off the desk and went to my knees in front of him, pulling my hair down from its bun. He wrapped it around his fist and tugged. I nearly moaned, the pinch of pain doing something to me I wasn't ready for.

"I used to have my nipples done, but some bras show them, and that's not great in a fight." He grunted as I swallowed him whole, and he began working in and out of my mouth. Even though I was the one keeping the pace, *he* was the one in control. Tricky bastard.

And then he moved faster, harder, and I hollowed my cheeks, doing my best not to gag as he hit the back of my throat. He wasn't rough, though, didn't make my eyes water, he just kept going. When he pulled away, I frowned up at him, licking my lips, reveling in the salty taste of his pre-come. He shook his head.

"If I finish now, I'm not going to come inside you. And that was the rule, wasn't it? For today only?"

I didn't recall if we had made that rule, but he was right. So, I looked down at his wet cock. "I don't have a condom."

He cursed under his breath before shucking out of his boots and pants quicker than I imagined. And then he went to another desk, his cock bobbing against his stomach, and it was all I could do not to jump him.

"Behold," he said as he pulled condoms from Noah's desk drawer.

I looked at him. "How on earth did you know they were there?"

"I found them by accident, and I don't ask Noah or Ford questions. You won't either."

I burst out laughing, but I nodded, and then I was on him. He caught me, and I wrapped my legs around him, careful to keep his cock away from my entrance. He wasn't covered, and there was no way that I was ready for that kind of risk.

He spread me across my desk, and I groaned as I watched him cover himself. When he was sheathed, he spread my legs, met my gaze, and thrust.

One time, no warning, just a deep breath and a stretch that was almost too much.

He met my gaze, and I knew if he didn't move soon, I would say something stupid.

Like something about emotions. And we weren't going to do that. We were friends who worked together. This was just for fun.

To satisfy the craving we'd had for the past year.

He leaned down and took my lips as if reading my mind, and then he moved. Hard and fast. I arched beneath him, needing him more than I thought possible. We were somehow on the floor, him taking the brunt of the fall.

"Oh my God, are you okay?"

"Just ride me, girl. I'll deal with the bruises later."

I laughed, I couldn't help it. And then I rode him, hands on his shoulders, ass up in the air as I moved up and down. He kept me steady, a bruising force I knew I would crave until the end of my days. Even if it was stupid.

He flipped me to all fours and got behind me, pummeling me. This was good because I couldn't meet his gaze. And he couldn't meet mine.

I was coming again, and he followed me. He didn't just roar my name. He whispered sweet nothings that *meant* nothing because they had to.

We collapsed, and I looked at him over my shoulder, his cock still pulsing inside me.

"Well, that's one way to end an assignment."

He grinned and shook his head, slowly working his way out of me. I knew I would be sore in the morning, yet it was what I yearned for.

"I should probably go deal with the cameras."

As soon as he said the words, I cursed and quickly sat up, not caring that I was naked in front of him. After all, he had just licked and touched every inch of me. "Fuck. How did we forget that?"

"Well, we're security specialists. Of course, we fucking forgot about the cameras."

I wanted to laugh at his sarcastic response, but a sense of urgency took over. I didn't need my friends and coworkers seeing my ass in the air as Gus pounded into me. No, thank you. "You take care of the condom and the main unit. I'll deal with the side one."

And with that, any romance or sexual tension between us burst because we had to clean up the evidence. Including the desk. The scent of sex was still in the air, and I had just fucked one of my best friends in our place of work, where anyone could have walked in.

In terms of mistakes in my life, this was a major one. Gus wasn't the mistake. I couldn't let him think he was either. Because that would be shitty for both of us. But when, where, why, and how? Yeah, those were the fucking mistakes.

Gus met my gaze after I slipped my shirt over my head.

"So. You okay?"

The joking part of me wanted to say, of course, then laugh it off and say we'd always be friends. That it wasn't him, and it wasn't me. It was just life.

But I met his gaze and knew this would become something we'd have to deal with. We didn't do relationships. We had work, friends, and nights of fun with others.

We didn't have commitments beyond our duty. Only this might change things.

"I'll see you tomorrow. Bright and early?"

"I can't wait for the full debrief," he said, the relief in his eyes hurting more than it should.

But when I held out my hand, he just rolled his eyes and shook it.

"Really? We're going to shake hands?"

"I don't know, it seemed right. After all, life moves on. But we scratched that itch, right?" I asked, my voice far too bright and cheery.

If he heard it, he didn't let on. He squeezed my hand, leaned forward, and kissed me softly on the cheek.

"I'll see you in the morning. And, Jen?"

I swallowed hard. "Yes?"

"You might always be a distraction, but that's on me. And you didn't fuck things up, I promise."

I stood frozen, wanting to say something. I couldn't want more from him, so I couldn't let myself feel. Therefore, in answer, I grabbed my things and let him follow me out after we closed down the shop.

We would move on. This was just one time, to get it out of our systems.

Moving on was what I was good at. It was what he was good at.

We wouldn't have any regrets.

I knew I was lying for both of us.

Chapter 3

Jennifer

2 Months Later

"Did you see this file?"

I looked up as Daisy walked over, her hair piled on the top of her head and dark circles under her eyes. She'd had a long night on a job, the client insisting they work overtime. They'd paid accordingly, but I wasn't sure how Daisy was here this morning. She must be exhausted. But she was the boss, and she didn't listen to anyone but herself when it came to her hours.

"I did. What's wrong, other than the normal?" I asked as I gestured toward the seat in front of me. She gave me a look but gingerly sat, favoring her leg again. She had been hurt in an explosion and kept saying she was fine, but we both knew she wasn't. And while Daisy was my friend, and I enjoyed spending time with her, she was also my boss, which meant I didn't get to kick her in the ass when she didn't take care of herself. Thankfully, she worked with her cousins, and they kicked her ass for me.

"There's a note here about the number of people they want on their detail. Isn't that up to us to decide?" she asked, her voice dry.

I cleared my throat as I looked over at Kate, our new admin. "Hey, Kate, can you repeat what the client said over the phone?"

Kate sighed. She was a recent hire and doing really well. She was about my age, with dark hair, bright eyes, and a strong work ethic. She also didn't take shit from anyone.

"Well, the client started off with certain demands, and while they sounded fine at first, they turned into insane requirements. Like no women were allowed to be part of the team. Then they wanted *all* women. And then they decided they wanted a mix and wanted to tell us exactly where we would be standing during certain events."

I looked over at Daisy, who hadn't been in the room for that phone call while Kate took notes, explained that wasn't how we worked, and then pulled her phone away from her ear so we could hear the screaming on the other end of the line.

"I'll handle it. And, Kate, the next time someone yells at you like that or has outrageous and sexist demands? You say the bosses will call them back and hang up. You are not paid to be emotionally abused by these fucking assholes. You got me?"

Kate nodded.

"Seriously, Kate. Our job is to find security threats for new buildings, install hardware and software, and be the point people for events. It's not to be yelled at because some egotistical asshole decides they know better."

"See?" Daisy said as she gestured toward me. "She understands."

Kate cleared her throat. "Oh, I understand. I just don't know if I'm allowed to yell back."

I laughed. "If they're in your face, do that sweet, casual, stern-talking you do."

I laughed at that, shaking my head. "Whenever I do that to one of our clients, they look at me like I've grown a second head. Because, apparently, I'm not allowed to string two words together without bending over so they can see my cleavage."

"People are such assholes," Daisy grumbled.

"Who are assholes now?" Kane walked in with a scowl and slid his phone into his pocket.

"Men," I said, fluttering my eyelashes. Kane rolled his eyes.

"Okay, now who's being sexist?"

"In this case, the clients," Daisy grumbled as she explained the phone call.

"I knew that client would be an issue, but Kingston thought we could handle it."

"I'm sure the guy was sweet and affable to you, one of the bros. But as soon as he heard that Daisy and I would be on the team and Kate's voice? Of course, he changed his tune. Because how could a little-bitty woman keep him safe?" I asked, pitching my voice slightly higher.

Kane held up both hands. "Do not bring me into that, but I can handle it."

"No, I will," Daisy said with a smile that scared me a bit. "Please, let me handle it."

Kane grinned. "Yes. Please, handle it. And record it so I can see the man crying."

"We don't make men cry," I put in. "Often."

"You know, I really like working here." Kate leaned her hand on the desk and smiled. "Seriously. You guys are like a big family and take care of each other. Much better than my old job."

"Much better than mine, too. And the bosses are okay." I winked at Daisy, who just grinned.

"I try my best not to be a jerk. Seriously, though, if people give you trouble, let us know. Most of our clients are nice. They're not assholes who think women should be in the kitchen."

"Damn straight. We both know you can't cook, Daisy," Kane said as he ducked the pen flying at him.

"What did I say about throwing things at work?" Noah asked.

Soon, everybody was there and it was a full house. I lifted my chin at Gus as he came to sit in his chair.

It had been two months since we'd slept together. And the fact that it had been the best sex of my life just meant I really needed to get out more. But we were still friends.

Because hot chemistry did not equal forever. And neither of us wanted that anyway.

It was better this way. We worked together, we still flirted, but the heat had died down. Just like we wanted. If it had been anything more, there would still be a connection between us. But we were just friends. And that was better for everyone.

I ignored the little kick in my gut.

"So, what'd we miss?" Gus asked before sipping his coffee. The guys had just come back from the bakery and coffee shop next door that Noah and Ford's woman owned. I was a little jealous that no one had brought me coffee, but I could walk over and get it myself later.

"Client X," Kate answered.

Gus winced. "Please, tell me I'm not on that detail. I mean, I cannot handle that guy."

"What did he do to you?" I asked.

Gus shook his head. "He's a leech. He's cheating on his wife and putting up cameras so he can make sure she's always on the other side of the house when he has his mistress over. That's going to get him caught."

"Excuse me?" I asked, rage sliding through me.

Gus held up his hands. "I'm not the one cheating. He is. And I feel like we're helping him."

Daisy stomped forward, the intense rage on her face apparent. "You know that for a fact? How did we miss it?" she asked Noah, who scowled at his computer.

"Because we weren't there for the install. It was Gus. Why the fuck didn't you tell us?"

"I was going to tell you today since it was just yesterday. And I didn't really want to say it over in the coffee shop." He looked at me. "By the way, Greer's working on a drink for you, but they had to fix one of the grinders. I didn't want the foam to die down by the time I got it to you. They'll bring it over in a minute."

For some reason, that felt weird to me. He hadn't even asked, yet made sure that the coffee I liked was on its way to me.

What the heck was wrong with me? This should be easy. We were friends. This is what we wanted.

And here he was, being helpful and getting me coffee without asking.

But that's what friends did. Right?

"Oh. Thanks. I was about to kick your ass for not bringing me anything." I winked as I said it, and Gus rolled his eyes.

"I know better than to stand between you and caffeine. They also had to open a new hazelnut flavoring pack since they had problems with inventory. You'll get your latte soon."

"What about me?" Daisy asked.

"I asked if you wanted coffee, and you said no," Noah said, scowling at his computer. "Let me deal with this client. We're going to bump him."

"I've got it," Daisy replied. As they bickered, I tried my best not to look at Gus.

Why was it so difficult? It shouldn't be this hard.

When Greer walked in, a four-pack of coffees in one hand and a bag of baked goods in the other, both Noah and Ford stopped arguing with Daisy and immediately brightened up, walking to their woman. They kissed as if they were in private, slowly but with a little heat. Greer staggered back, blushing, while the guys took the baked goods and coffees from her. I did my best not to feel jealous.

Greer was an amazing person. She had been through a lot recently, as well as during her childhood, so the fact that she was so happy right now meant the world. She deserved it. She deserved two men who would do anything for her. Who looked at her like she was the center of their universe.

Once again, I did my best not to look over at Gus. That would be ridiculous.

"I just saw you like ten minutes ago." Greer shook her head with a smile. "But I brought coffee."

"Thank you so much," I said, walking over to take my latte from Ford. "You didn't have to do that."

"It gave me an excuse to take a walk since I don't do it enough."

"How many steps do you get in a day working at the coffee place?" Noah asked with a frown. "How can you not walk enough?"

"I was in the office all day yesterday, so I felt like I needed the workout."

"Oh, we could get a workout in," Ford said, and everybody groaned.

"I really don't need to hear these things," Daisy said from the other side of the office.

"Seriously. This is your workplace. You're the boss. Act like it," Kane said, though he was grinning from ear to ear.

I looked at Kate, who smiled at me and rolled her eyes, and I knew she'd fit right in.

We'd had a few admins over the past year, and none of them worked. Either they didn't want to do their job, or they thought it was a stepping stone to ours. And while we were always open to using more contract workers, we needed someone who excelled at organizing us. Because Noah couldn't do it all, especially when he had a life outside this place.

I liked that as Kate learned the ropes, she ensured we were always where we needed to be. I felt safer because of it. Our jobs weren't always dangerous, but they sometimes were, and that meant I needed to trust everyone on my team.

I took my coffee and pastry back to my desk as everyone grabbed theirs, then returned to work, studying my next assignment. I did mainly installations these days, but I was also on bodyguard duty.

It wasn't always for celebrities. Sometimes, it was just for a CEO at an event. Other times, it was for a person who'd been threatened. You couldn't help when danger came at you. It was our job to protect them.

We all settled down. Noah and Ford left to meet with new clients. Another client came in, and Kane and Kingston took him to a more private area. I had a few certifications coming up and a couple of additional classes I wanted to take, which meant busy days. But I liked my work.

I liked the people I worked with.

And I liked Gus.

When everyone returned from lunch, I realized I hadn't taken my break and cursed at myself. I was starving, and the pastry was long gone, so when I stood up quickly, it shouldn't have been a surprise that I got lightheaded. I needed to eat, especially because of my workouts. It was important for me to keep my calorie intake up. I shook my head, trying to will the dizziness away.

"Jen?" Gus asked as he came over. I held out my hand.

"I stood up too fast and didn't eat lunch. I'm going to go take care of that at the café. Do you want anything?"

He studied my face. I wasn't sure what he saw. I also wasn't sure I liked that he could read me so well.

"Are you sure you're okay?"

"I'm fine. Promise. Actually, since it's so late in the day, I might go pick up my food and head to my class for the afternoon." I turned to Daisy. "Is that all right?"

"I was going to suggest that since I noticed you skipped lunch. Don't do that again, missy."

My lips twitched, but I nodded before grabbing my things and heading out. I didn't have an install or a client today, but I did have a few classes.

I picked up my lunch, a little dizzy and still slightly woozy. Even the thought of my sandwich didn't sit well.

So weird. I didn't get sick like this. I had an iron stomach, at least according to my family.

I started on my way home. My head hurt, and I realized I was going to throw up. I quickly pulled into the parking lot of a grocery store, opened the door, and emptied my stomach. Shaky, my palms damp, I reached for the water I always had with me and chugged it.

"What the hell?"

I didn't think it was anything I'd eaten. But still, this wasn't normal. I thought about what I had in my house and realized I needed to get some things for my stomach at the grocery store. I made my way inside, grabbed a few antacids, and then paused, doing the math.

No, it totally isn't that. It can't be that. No.

As I made my way down the next aisle, I grabbed a pregnancy test, just in case. It never hurt to be safe. Except that we had been safe. Very safe.

I was on birth control, and we'd used a condom. It was probably just a stomach bug.

I checked out and drove home, doing the math, worries whirling in my brain. I needed to head to my class. I didn't have time for my overactive imagination.

However, instead of taking the antacids, I shakily made my way to my restroom and took a test I knew would come out negative. I would fail it—or pass it, whatever lingo worked best for that. And I would move on.

I paced my tiny bathroom, pretending to look at social media on my phone as I waited.

I turned toward the bathroom sink, the test stick on the edge of the counter, and set down my phone.

Pregnant.

Vivid dark words on a white display.

Pregnant.

Well, then.

I leaned over the toilet and threw up.

Chapter 4

Gus

"This is a one-and-a-half-pound piece of whirling wood and metal, and yet it feels more powerful," Kane said as he held up the ax, grinning at me.

"See, I don't think it's smart to have beer at a place where you throw axes."

Kane rolled his eyes. "Excuse me, I'm not drunk. I haven't even had a sip of my beer. This is why we do this, and *then* we go drink. It's what guys' nights are for."

Kane turned, moved into position, did exactly what our instructors told us, and tossed the ax. It whirled in the air, a perfect toss, and hit the bullseye. It landed with a satisfying thud, and Kane raised his hands and cheered.

I just shook my head. "That's it. Next time, I'm on your team."

"Damn straight. You never go against a Montgomery."

"I thought his last name was Carr?" my brother Sawyer asked.

Kingston laughed. "His mom is the Montgomery, so Montgomery is his middle name. It doesn't matter that his last name is Carr. When in the vicinity of the Montgomerys, you become one. It's a cult."

Sawyer gave me a wide-eyed look, and I snorted. "It's okay. I promise I'm not in a cult."

"I feel like that's exactly what someone in a cult would say," my brother said, and I laughed.

"Come on, you're up next."

"I don't know. I feel like we should just go have a beer and let them win."

"I don't think so," Ford said. "We have an hour and a half of practice, and then we have the tournament."

"They have a tournament every night? How is it a tournament, then?" Sawyer asked, ever the analytical man.

"It's like trivia night. You have a winner for the evening. And unless you're part of a team that regularly goes against another and keeps score, it's just for the night. I promise. It's not insane."

"You say that, but we're throwing axes. When did this become a thing?"

"I'm sure some celebrity did it and then put it on social media. And here we are," Noah said as he looked up from his phone.

"Are you texting Greer? I thought this was supposed to be a man's night."

"It's a guys' night. If you say man's night, it sounds like we're going to puff up our chests and compare dicks," Kane said as he sat back down when Sawyer went to take his turn.

I snorted, grateful I hadn't taken a sip of my drink.

"Well, I didn't hit anyone. I'm going to count that as a win," Sawyer said as he came back to sit next to me. I looked at the ax embedded in the wall, a foot to the left of the target.

"You did better when there were multiple targets with the ducks. You know, where you could hit the one on the left like you constantly do."

"You're placating me. Maybe I should go have a drink."

"You're welcome to it," Ford said. "Most people are having a drink or two while out here. We never do, but only because we usually do this on work nights."

"I guess that's true. No one needs a hangover in your line of business." Sawyer paused. "Or any line of business."

"Damn straight," I said. "Seriously, though, the tournament is soon. Are you ready?"

Ford frowned. "I feel like the training session was too quick. The group games are fun, but for a winner-take-all tournament? I'm a little worried."

"It's fine. We've got this," I said with a laugh, though I wasn't sure I truly believed it. Kane and Kingston were really good at this, probably the best in the room. But Ford and Noah were too busy texting Greer to really put their hearts into it. Sawyer was a lost cause, and I was off my game. I just wouldn't think about *why*.

"Okay, get ready, the Tournament of Teams is about to begin," a man declared via the intercom before going over the rules.

Sawyer sighed. "I'm not ready."

"It's okay. Maybe you'll do better when it counts," Kane said kindly.

"I really don't believe that."

I grinned. "It's fine. We have to hit targets for some of our qualifications. And a lot of us have experience throwing things."

"I was a pitcher in high school," Ford said with a grin.

"Now you pitch other things," Noah said with a smirk, and Ford leaned down and pressed a kiss to his lips.

"Shut up," Ford grumbled, his cheeks going red.

I laughed, the others joining in.

"I did not need to know who the catcher was in that situation," Kane said lightheartedly.

"I'm learning so many new things. Thanks for taking me out, brother," Sawyer said with a laugh, his eyes dancing.

"Okay, Team Montgomery, here we are," the man over the intercom said, and Sawyer and I met gazes before bursting out laughing.

"Did we pick the team name?" Kane asked. "Because it'd be nice to use my real name for once. Just saying."

Ford flipped him off. "I'll have you know I'm not a Montgomery either."

"No, you're just living, sleeping, and going to marry one," Noah said drily.

Ford shrugged. "Yes. And figuring out the last names for the three of us when all of us have families we actually like? That is going to be fun."

"I don't envy you in the least," I put in. "Seriously, though, why change your names?"

"Because it'll make things easier for paperwork and power of attorneys when it comes to kids," Noah put in.

I nodded. "I guess you're right. But maybe the power of attorney will be enough."

"Thankfully, we know a few lawyers," Ford said dryly. Considering his family, that made sense.

By the time I got my turn, I wanted to kick the other team's ass. They were a bunch of jerks, glaring at Ford and Noah, and we all knew why. Homophobic assholes existed everywhere, and ax throwing while drinking beer did not cure them of that.

I tossed the ax. And hit the bullseye, the light above it going red. We all cheered as I lifted my chin at the asshole who had muttered something derogatory at Noah. The other man flipped me off before snarling something under his breath at Ford.

"Just ignore them," Noah mumbled.

"I'm working on it," I said. "I hate the fact that you have to deal with it."

Noah shrugged. "You get over it. Because then you get to kick their ass in little ways. Like in this tournament."

"Well, that means I need to step up my game," Sawyer said with a growl. "Because there's no way they're going to beat us. Even if I'm the weak link."

"Then go kick some ass," Kane encouraged.

Sawyer rolled his shoulders back and let the ax fly. When it hit the bullseye and the alarm went off, we just stared at each other until he jumped up, his fist in the air. We all cheered.

With the tournament over, and the Montgomery team winning, of course, we sat back in the corner, beers in hand, chomping on pretzel bites with beer cheese and a pizza that looked semi-edible.

"I think this was frozen at one point," Kane said.

I swallowed a decent bite of pizza. "True. The food isn't great, and the beer's slightly warm, but it's been fun."

Kingston looked around, his eyes narrowed. "I bet we could open one of our own."

"What? With all the spare time you have owning a security business?" I asked, taking a sip of my beer.

Kingston shrugged. "If not me, then one of the family members."

"So, is this an empire taking over the world, or a cult?" Sawyer asked.

I burst out laughing, shaking my head. "I think it's both."

Kane tilted his beer toward me, eyebrow raised. "You know none of you are wrong. But we could open something like this. Attach it to a game center for families, too. Or, I don't know, someplace where people could have fun but not be idiots."

I knew who he was glaring at—the guys behind us who were getting drunker by the minute. Thankfully, it seemed the owners had noticed and were coming over to talk to them. Wouldn't *that* be fun when we walked out later?

"You okay?" I asked.

Noah shrugged. "We're used to it. At least Greer isn't here. I hate when she has to take the brunt of the looks."

"People still weird about the poly thing?" I asked, my voice low.

Noah leaned forward. "Yeah, and while Ford and I do our best to ignore it, Greer can't. It hits her hard. Even if she puts on a brave face."

Ford signed. "And we can't just go out and kick someone's ass every time we want to."

"Nope, but we can change the way we feel about it," Noah added. "Though that is easier said than done."

I nodded as I sipped my beer. "If I ever see it around me, though, I'll do my best to make sure it doesn't happen twice."

Noah nodded. "I know. Everyone in our building knows. We have good people around. Unlike before." A dark cloud crossed over his eyes, and I knew what he remembered. Something none of us wanted to talk about.

"But the gallery's up, the café's doing great, and the tattoo shop's kicking ass with a huge waiting list. And we're not doing too bad ourselves."

"Again, Montgomerys taking over the world," Kane said with a grin.

"And, apparently, you're adding an ax shop to it," I added.

"Or at least something with better food," Kingston mumbled, taking notes.

I didn't know which would be better: notes for the job, or perhaps actual plans for taking over the world. Suddenly, he smiled softly, and I realized it wasn't any of that. It was a woman. Interesting. I hadn't known he was seeing anyone. From the curious look on Kane's face, he hadn't known either.

"So, you ever going to tell us what happened between you and Jennifer?" Kane asked out of the blue, startling me.

Sawyer leaned forward. "Jennifer? The woman he works with and never stops talking about? That Jennifer?" my brother asked.

I flipped him off. "Subtle. Real subtle."

"Yes, I'd like to know, too," Noah added.

"We're friends. We're coworkers. It would get messy if it was anything more."

Both Noah and Ford looked at each other, then at me. "Yes. It gets messy. But as long as it's consensual and doesn't bleed into work, it wouldn't be a problem. We honestly don't care as long as you don't hurt anyone. That's our goal with anything," Noah said.

I swallowed hard. "Just friends. That's all we want."

"Are you sure about that?" Kane asked. I glared at him, but thankfully our check came.

We pushed the subject to the side, though I knew my brother and my coworkers would bring it up again later. And I'd have to find a real answer for them.

We all headed out, my brother leaving first since he had an early morning. As we made it to the cars, Noah cursed under his breath.

"I knew they hadn't left quietly," Noah mumbled.

I turned around and cursed right along with him. "Well, hell."

"Aren't we too old for this?" Kingston asked.

"Hey, assholes. You really think you can get us kicked out of our favorite joint?" one of the guys slurred.

"I'm pretty sure you did that yourself," I put in.

"Let's not get them any angrier than they already are. I'm not in the mood to deal with the cops tonight," Noah said.

"It would be nice to kick their asses, though. Again," Ford said.

"Fuck you." The man leered at Ford and then said a word that made me want to kick his ass to make sure he never said it again. He staggered forward, fist out. Ford easily ducked, and I moved quickly, taking the man's wrist and twisting his arm behind his back. I bent him over so he couldn't try to hit anyone again.

"You're going to want to stop doing that."

"Fuck you. Get your hands off me."

"Don't you dare touch my friend!" the other drunk guy slurred as he came forward, fists moving quickly toward the guys.

The group was drunk, ignorant, and made of dumbasses, especially going against people who were highly trained and could deescalate without violence. So, we did. We moved, pinning them to their cars.

Ford sighed. "It would've been nice to punch the asshole in the face, but no, we're going to deal with it like adults."

When the owner of the ax-throwing place stormed out, he took one look at us and rolled his eyes.

"I should have known you'd take care of it. I'm sorry. I thought they left. They moved their cars around to the side where I couldn't see."

"You want us to call the authorities?" Noah asked. When the owner sighed and nodded, I knew it would be a long night.

"I don't want them out there drinking and driving. Or hurting somebody because they're pissed off."

"Fuck you. They're the ones hurting us," the guy I was holding snapped.

"We both know that's not the case, Chris." The owner sighed again and ran his hands over his hair for the umpteenth time.

It had been a good night until this. We'd played, and I'd hung out with my brother, which I rarely did these days, And I had totally lied about only wanting Jennifer to be my friend.

Things were going great.

When the cops arrived, I let the guy go. I pulled out my phone to check the time, definitely not looking for a text. Or a call. We didn't really do that. We used to text, flirt, joke. But things had changed. That fire had sizzled out. At least, that's what I told myself. It's what I *had* to tell myself.

I hadn't realized how quickly I'd fallen for Jennifer. My friend.

But she wasn't mine, and I had to remember that.

Even if it was getting harder to do each day.

Chapter 5

Gus

"I've got a bad feeling about this."

I turned to Kane and frowned. "Are you quoting *Star Wars* now?" I asked, my voice slow and sarcastic. Although he wasn't wrong. I had a bad feeling about it, too.

We were nearing the end of an event for around six hundred people with a few guest speakers and lots of wining and dining. Elbows rubbed, palms smoothed. All that crap.

I didn't mind what people did at these things, but this one felt off. As if there was something I wasn't getting. That worried me.

We were security for the event as a whole, not for any individual person. Making sure people were safe and any threats were taken care of. We had contract workers with us because it was a big enough event that we wanted to ensure we had coverage.

"So, why do we all have a bad feeling about this?" Jennifer asked as she walked over.

I turned toward her, keeping my voice low. "I don't know. Something feels off."

Alert, she gave me a tight nod before looking out over the crowd. She moved on slowly, keeping on patrol with Daisy. My job was to stay in place near the doors unless there was an emergency.

The interaction between Jennifer and I had been easy, which I was grateful for. Because, frankly, things had been awkward lately. We had been fine these past two months. Yes, there was still heat, that connection, but I thought perhaps it had been toned down because we'd finally let it burn for a night. It wasn't everything. It wasn't what it could be, but we'd had each other.

Yet it felt as if we had screwed up.

Because something had changed the past few days. There was a rigidity to her, and she wouldn't quite meet my eyes.

Something was wrong, and I didn't know what I had done. But we needed to fix it. Especially because we fucking worked together. That was the whole point of us having the talk about our relationship to begin with.

People depended on us.

"I am glad this part of the day is almost over," Kane mumbled as he moved back to his position, eyes on the crowd. I nodded, though he couldn't see me, that itch still underneath my shoulder blades.

"Too bad it's a two-day event," I mumbled.

"Keep the lines clear," Noah said into the mic, but I could hear the frustration in his tone. He felt it, too. Whatever this was.

This was our final job with these clients. The team kept making changes, which we agreed to, but it caused us to have to double up or alter how we worked. They also wanted us to have one-on-one time with some of the heavy hitters, which would've been fine, but they had requested Daisy and Jennifer specifically. It set my teeth on edge. The one who had suggested it was lucky I hadn't punched him in the face, and that was only after hearing about it secondhand. Somehow, Ford had been able to hold back.

We had to finish this contract. One more day, and then we were done.

Then maybe I could figure out what the hell was going on with Jennifer and how to fix it.

And tell her that I wanted something more.

Which was great. Because I was pretty sure she wanted nothing to do with me.

That wouldn't make things hard at all.

"I'm just saying, you'd be great working in private security, don't you think?" a man slurred quietly over our earpieces. I frowned, wondering who the hell that was. Instincts on alert, I looked over and saw Daisy and Jennifer standing straight-backed, glaring at a man between them.

"Sir, you're going to want to give us some space," Jennifer said calmly.

"Are you sure you want space, baby? The two of you would be perfect with me. Private security? All the bonuses you could want. Get you out of this lifestyle and into the one you deserve. Don't you think?"

He reached for Daisy with one hand, Jennifer with the other, and I took a step forward before I could stop myself. Kane cleared his throat and shook his head because we weren't about to make a scene, and Noah was already on his way.

Plus, the women didn't need us. Not in this case.

"Touch me, and I'll break your fingers," Daisy said sweetly, so much so it made me stiffen.

"You wouldn't hurt me."

"We would. We'd make a scene, and we'd make sure everyone knew you're a creep. Because I don't think you'd like two *little girls* beating your ass. Now, you're going to step away and let us do our job, or we're going to show you exactly what private security means," Jennifer said, just as sweetly as Daisy.

"Bitch," the man grumbled just as Noah got there, a pleasant smile on his face and danger in his eyes. The fact that I could see that from this side of the room told me he was ready to kick ass. As were all of us.

"Sir, why don't you come with me?"

"I don't have to go with you anywhere."

"Oh, you're going to want to," Daisy added. "Because if you stay with us any longer, you'll be missing your balls."

Jennifer grinned before looking over the man's shoulder at me. She winked, and it felt like everything was normal again. Only maybe it wasn't. I wanted to help her, but she could take care of herself. I had to remember that.

The man sauntered off, practically swaggering, but he'd gotten his ego hit. I hoped he didn't fuck up anything later.

"We're wrapping up. Get to your positions, and then we'll have a briefing to set up for tomorrow," Ford said into the comms. I went back to work, pulling my gaze from Jennifer—something that was getting harder and harder to do.

When we headed back to the cars, the evening wrapped up, I looked over at Jennifer. "You okay?"

She raised a brow, and I noticed that she was a bit pale. Hell. Maybe the guy had gotten to her after all.

"I'm used to men hitting on me in these situations. They see a woman who can beat their ass and think they want it. Then they realize they can't handle it."

"They never can," Daisy mumbled before getting into the back of the SUV, Kane joining her.

I met Jennifer's gaze. "I'm sorry."

"Don't be. You don't treat women like that. You treat me like a member of the team. One of the guys. And I appreciate that."

I raised a brow, grateful that our comms were off. "You know I don't treat you like one of the guys."

Her eyes darkened for a bit before she suddenly paled even further.

"No, I guess you don't. And, Gus? We need to talk after this whole event's over."

My stomach rolled, but I nodded, my jaw tightening. "Yeah. It seems we do."

She met my gaze again and looked like she wanted to say something more before changing her mind and getting into the SUV. I sighed, heading to the other one.

This wouldn't end well.

* * * *

The next day was more of the same, although I was worried about what she had to say.

But I had to put it in the back of my mind because we were almost done with this assignment.

"I'm really glad we're not working with this client after this," Jennifer said with a sigh, rubbing the back of her neck.

We were in the corner of the room, keeping track of the exits. I frowned at her. "Why do you say that?"

"The creep you heard yesterday was just the tip of the iceberg. I'm surprised no one's propositioned you yet." I winced, and she narrowed her eyes. "Seriously?"

"Seriously. I don't know what's going on with this client, but I don't like it."

"Tell Noah."

"I don't need to complain to Noah about a woman asking me to show her what her pearl necklace could look like." Jennifer choked. "Pretend I didn't say that out loud."

"Are you fucking kidding me right now? She said that? Blatantly?"

"It was when we were setting up for the day. She's one of the organizers."

"If you don't tell Noah, I will."

"It'll be handled."

"Do it. Please? I don't want to think about what else these people are doing if they're being so blunt with us."

"We can't do much about it, other than not work with them anymore."

"What if they do it to someone else? To the next team? We need to get them blacklisted or something."

I snorted, even as she glared at me.

"What? Am I insane for wanting to take care of my friends and family?"

That was Jennifer—sweet and caring, even when she wanted to kick ass.

I wanted us to be okay. To get back to normal. Or maybe as soon as we talked, things would deteriorate again.

"We'll work on it after. But let's keep our eyes on the prize. We're almost done."

"Don't say things like that. It's just going to jinx it."

"Yeah. I'll go throw salt over my shoulder."

"You should go run around the building three times," she said with a laugh.

I shook my head, holding back a laugh of my own. "Let's not do that. I'm not in the mood to get yelled at by Noah again."

"Again? What did you do this time?"

"Nothing. I was a perfect angel."

She rolled her eyes, and we went back to work. I felt lighter than I had in days. *This* was what I'd missed, the normalcy of it all.

"Hey, we have a problem," Noah said. I cursed myself as Jen gave me a look, waiting to hear if I truly had jinxed us.

"What is it?"

"It seems some people the organizer apparently threatened online last night threatened him back. And mentioned this place specifically."

I thought back, trying to remember what had been said while Jen pulled up her phone. She paled.

"Well, hell. This group is known for being good at explosives and weaponry. They're on watch lists around the country."

She turned the screen to me, and I cursed a blue streak in my head.

"Shit."

"We're on it. Kingston's searching the floors now. But be on the ball. I don't like it. I don't like it at all."

"Same. This feels wrong."

"We're on it, keep alert. Let's just get this done," Noah growled. We spread out, keeping our head in the game. Though it wasn't easy, not when it was all I could do not to pick up Jennifer and get her the hell out of there. I did not know how Noah and Ford did it. I didn't know what I would do if Jen got hurt. And that's when I knew I'd made a fucking mistake by sleeping with her. It would've been easier to walk away before that. Now, there was no going back.

We kept on alert. A few of the guests might've noticed, but they were too busy having fun, making deals, laughing, and ignoring the fact that we were searching the building for a bomb.

One that never should have gotten in. But if it was small enough? There were always ways. Especially in a building like this, with so many crevices and entrances and exits. It was one of the things we hadn't liked about the event.

But the company wanted this, and we'd had to make concessions.

I didn't think we'd be doing that again. Ever.

"I don't like this," Jennifer whispered next to me, and I nodded in agreement.

"I should have run around the building."

"There's still time."

But I realized maybe we didn't have the time.

I saw something small and metallic in a guy's hands. A small pipe bomb, which wouldn't do too much damage—except to the person standing right next to it.

Jen saw him at the same time, Kingston coming up behind him fast.

When the guy threw it, I didn't think. I pulled Jennifer back, throwing my body over hers as the bomb hit the wall beside us and everything went dark.

Chapter 6

Jennifer

Screaming. So much damn screaming. That was all I could hear with Gus on top of me, my instincts telling me to push him off and find the assailant. Yet the rest of me raged to make sure he was okay.

I could feel his breath on my neck, so I knew he was alive, but from the blood pooling beneath us, I also knew he was hurt.

So stupid. The man was so stupid. And I was also stupid for nearly falling in love with him—something I wasn't going to let myself dwell on as the world burned around me. I had to make sure he was okay. I needed to ensure that my team was all right.

Things moved quickly after that, with Noah and Ford pulling Gus off me, and Daisy taking my hand.

"Are you okay?"

I put my other hand over my stomach, aware that it wasn't just me. I needed to tell the team. Because it wasn't just me anymore.

Daisy's gaze went to my hand, her eyes wide, and I shook my head. I felt fine. Gus had even cushioned me from the fall the best he could with his arms. I wouldn't forgive him if he got hurt because of me.

I would never forgive him for that.

"Gus?"

My heart raced, and I bent down, cupping his cheek. There was blood beneath him, but I couldn't see where it was coming from. Why did he throw himself on top of me like that?

He had to be okay.

"Let's get you checked out."

"What happened after we fell?" I asked, trying to clear my head. Daisy pulled me away from Gus. I tried to stop her, but the others were there, and she was checking me out. She was certified in emergency first aid and could help, but all I wanted to do was get to Gus.

Because he wasn't moving.

"It was one man," Daisy said, keeping her gaze on mine. When her attention moved down to my stomach again, I shook my head. I didn't want anyone else to know. The fact that she knew from that one hand movement told me how close we were. The problem was, I knew Gus would also figure it out. Because we were that close, too. It didn't matter that he didn't have the feminine intuition Daisy had. He would know.

I needed him to be okay.

I tried to look behind me, but Daisy took my face in her hands and forced me to look at her.

"Talk to me."

"We saw the man coming through the east door. I don't know what tipped Gus off, but I moved at the same time he did, trying to get to him. Kingston was behind him."

I tried to look for Kingston, but Daisy wouldn't let me move my head. "And?"

"I don't know. The guy threw the bomb. I don't even know what kind it was. I couldn't exactly see what was in his hand. But then Gus threw himself on top of me."

Rage and worry warred with each other. Worry for Gus. The baby. Everyone.

"Why would he do that?" I asked, my voice shaking. "He shouldn't have done that. I would've been fine."

"Does he know?" Daisy asked, her voice low.

I shook my head. Of course, she knew it was Gus's. She figured it out just by looking at me.

"Okay. Kingston's fine. He tackled the guy. Everyone's being evacuated. We're searching for more explosives, and the authorities are here, including the bomb squad. It'll be out of our hands soon."

I nodded, knowing Noah would have a headache to face with the paperwork.

"And Gus?" I asked, swallowing hard.

"They're putting him in the ambulance right now."

I whirled away from her. My fear had let her keep me from seeing him. There was still blood on the floor where he had covered my body with his, and the bomb had taken out the wall, or at least part of it. But that was mostly it. Tables were overturned beyond that, but from what I could tell, it was because of people running, not the bomb.

I looked around, checking for any other injuries, trying to get a sense of what the hell had happened, but I couldn't. Our team was working like they should, getting everybody out. And I was here with Daisy because she hadn't wanted me to see Gus being taken away.

"Was he awake? Was he alert?"

She didn't say anything for a moment, and I knew that was an answer in itself.

"We need to go to the hospital. *I* need to go to the hospital."

"Yes, you do. Because we need to get you checked out. You were knocked out, too."

"I didn't lose consciousness," I snapped.

"But we both know you need to go." She tapped her earpiece, and I knew we were being recorded. I didn't need the team to know I was pregnant before I had a chance to tell Gus.

I needed to be able to tell Gus. He had to know.

"Let's get you to the hospital to get checked out, and then we'll see Gus. He's going to be fine."

"Why did he do that? Why did he push me out of the way? I would've been fine."

"I think you need to ask him that."

"He broke protocol."

Daisy shook her head vehemently. "Protocol is to stay alive. We're not the Secret Service here. Yes, we have to protect our charges, but we have to be alive in order to do that."

"I need him to wake up and have the doctors tell us he's all clear."

"Of course. And then we're going to have a talk." She glared at me, and I nodded.

Pregnant women were of course allowed to work for the company. First, it would be illegal if we weren't, and second, the Montgomerys were a breeding family. My lips twitched at that thought, even with the situation. Because they were constantly having children. Daisy had like ninety cousins and second cousins. And all of them came from families who owned businesses. They worked hard, played harder, and took care of their own no matter what. But we were the first security company in the family. I might not be a Montgomery by birth, but they had taken me in when I joined the company, and I counted them as friends. But being pregnant while in the line of duty where my unborn child could get hurt was a risk I wasn't sure I could take. I had wanted to talk it out with Gus and my team before making any decisions. Today should have been easy. It should have been an in-and-out. Nobody should have gotten hurt.

"Let's go. Noah and Ford have it," Kane snapped, glaring. "That was a clusterfuck. We never should have taken this job."

"Any word on Gus?" I asked, my words coming fast.

"No." He froze when he got a good look at me. "You've got blood on you. Is it yours?"

I shook my head, feeling slightly woozy. Then again, I'd been feeling that way for the past few days.

"No, I'm fine. Maybe a bruise from hitting the ground, but Gus took the brunt of the damage from above. He's going to make it through this."

"Damn straight. Crap," Kane growled, and we made our way to the SUV.

The authorities stopped us, and I sighed, wanting to get to the hospital, to get to Gus. But first, we had some questions to answer. People to deal with.

And a shit ton of paperwork to come.

I hoped he would be fine. No, he would make it.

Because there wasn't another outcome. I would never forgive myself if it happened any other way.

I let out a deep breath and swore I would yell at him for putting himself in danger for me. And then I would tell him everything, even if it broke me.

But first, he needed to wake up.

* * * *

"Let's get you checked out," Daisy said after a minute, but I shook my head, pacing the hospital waiting room.

Once we'd finished with the authorities, we made our way to the emergency room. I was the worst off, covered in dust and blood. The nurse had taken one look at me and decided that I needed to go back to see someone. I shook them off, saying it wasn't my blood and that I was fine. I just wanted to hear about Gus. However, since we weren't family, and Gus hadn't told them or been able to tell them that we were allowed to hear any information, it was a waiting game. We literally had no idea what was going on back there, only that he was at this hospital.

"Are you sure no one else was hurt?" I asked as Kingston rubbed the back of his neck.

"No one else was hurt. I'm just pissed off that I didn't see the guy in time. That he was able to get the dumbass homemade bomb in at all."

I continued to pace as Daisy stood against the wall, watching me as if

I might fall at any moment. I didn't blame her because I *was* still slightly woozy. Noah and Ford were still on-site, as were a few of our other team members. Kingston had come with us because he had watched the wall come down over us. I was fine. Not even a bruise—at least yet. All because Gus had taken the brunt of it. I was going to kick his ass. He was not allowed to sacrifice himself for me. Who the hell did he think he was?

"He got through because his cousin worked at the hotel. Apparently, they look enough alike that he got past our contract worker." Daisy snarled the last words, and I knew Noah and Ford were dealing with whoever had made the mistake. We were human, it happened, but Gus had gotten hurt. And I knew nothing about what was going on back there.

My phone rang, making my heart race, somehow thinking it was Gus calling me from the other side of the double doors they'd barred us from.

But no, it was my mother. I didn't want to talk to her right now. Not because I didn't love her, but because she had probably heard about the incident on the news. And I hadn't called her.

"Answer. I already have the family group chat on alert because they're afraid I'm going to get myself blown up again. Thankfully, it was just you this time," Daisy said lightly, but I heard the hurt behind it. She had nearly been killed. And Kingston had been there, nearly getting hurt himself. Their families had been through so much, while mine was relatively normal. Their daughter just happened to like putting herself on the line.

But I was pregnant now. Which meant I needed to think about what I was doing with my life.

I answered as I moved off to the side, trying my best to keep some things quiet.

"Are you okay, Jennifer?" my mother asked, and I realized she was on speakerphone.

"I'm fine. I don't know what I'm allowed to talk about, other than the fact that nobody died." Because Gus was fine. He was alive. I would know if he wasn't. "I'm still waiting to hear about Gus, though."

"Gus? Oh, no. Do you want us to be there with you so you're not alone?" my sister asked. She was infatuated with Gus. She was a decade younger than me and still a baby to me.

"He's going to be fine. We're just waiting to hear details."

"If you say so," she said.

"Are you okay? Did you get checked out?" my dad asked, his voice low.

Tears came to my eyes, and I swallowed them down. I loved my family. They were strong, caring, and had no idea what to do with me most days. I had been out there climbing trees and jumping off roofs as a little girl, wanting to play with the boys in the neighborhood, when my mom had only wanted me to stay safe. She hadn't wanted me inside playing with dolls or cleaning the house and baking cookies. No, she'd wanted me to live my life and have fun, but I usually tried to live it to the limit.

I put my hand over my stomach, my voice shaky as I explained to them that I was fine and would update them soon.

Because I was pregnant. I was going to be a mom. This little baby would likely grow up to be a person who jumped off roofs and put themselves in danger. Both of their parents were like that. Gus was wild but tried to be safe. Yet he always put himself at the forefront. He sacrificed his body to protect me, despite the fact that I could protect myself. He had safeguarded the child he didn't even know existed.

I needed to tell him. And I would. I was just so damn afraid of what would happen.

I didn't even know where we stood in our relationship. We were friends who had decided it would be too complicated to want more. Not that we didn't *want* more, but because we didn't want the complications.

Well, here was one hell of a complication. A consequence of our actions. Ones that had been some of the best of my life. But now we needed to figure out what the hell we were going to do.

"Jennifer?"

I whirled to see Sawyer, Gus's brother, and tears sprang to my eyes. "Is he awake?"

Sawyer ran his hands through his hair. "He texted me. That's all I know."

I looked at my phone, looking for a message that wasn't there. I ignored the twinge of pain at that, considering he'd texted his brother. "He's okay? He was the one who texted? Not someone with his phone?"

"I think so. He said he was fine. You're not in the back with him?" he asked, before seeming to understand the answer. "Because you're not family. Fuck. Okay, I'll go see what I can do. I'll get you back there, I promise." He looked me up and down and frowned. "Are you okay? Have you been checked out?"

For some reason, tears began falling then, and I just threw my hands around Gus's brother and held on tight. "I'm fine. But your dumbass brother threw himself on top of me. Protected me from the blast."

Sawyer held me tightly. I took a step back, just as he did, trying to catch my breath. I was shaky, but it had nothing to do with the pregnancy. It was the adrenaline rushing through my body.

"That sounds like Gus. Let me go see him. If they let me. And then I'll go kick his ass for sacrificing himself, then hug him for doing that and protecting you, then kick his ass more for not texting you."

"Yes, he should text us. We're all waiting out here. And those who aren't here are dealing with the situation and waiting for updates, too."

"I'm on it. The whole family is on their way. Their drive's just a little bit longer." I remembered then that Gus's family lived in Castle Rock, so the drive up I-25 would be terrible at this time of day.

"Just let me know. I'll update the others with this little bit of information."

Sawyer shook his head. "I'm sure he wants to know you're okay too, you know."

"Then go kick his ass so I can do it."

"I knew I always liked you." He walked through the doors, and I turned towards Kingston and Daisy, who stared at me, hands on their hips. They never looked more like cousins than in that moment.

"So?"

"He texted his brother. I don't know what else."

"Well. At least that's something." Kingston let out a deep breath before sinking into the chair, hands over his face. Daisy began to pace, cursing under her breath.

"Why the hell didn't he text us? Or let them know?"

A nurse came out at that moment, looking a little harried and wide-eyed. "Is someone out here named Jennifer? There's a very large man growling and wondering why you aren't by his bedside." She rolled her eyes as relief flooded my body.

"Is his name Gus?"

"I think that was thrown about in the growling."

"Is he okay?" I blurted as Daisy and Kingston came to my sides.

"He can answer that for himself. Come on down. I'll show you." She looked at the other two behind me. "I'm sorry, he already has one visitor. You'll have to take turns."

"Just keep us updated," Daisy ordered, and I nodded. "And get checked out yourself."

The nurse gave me a knowing look. "You're covered in dirt and blood. I assume that's not yours?"

"It's from the big man who's currently growling."

"That makes sense. Though you should change."

"I'll get you some clothes," Daisy said, pulling out her phone.

"We have some scrubs for you, too, just in case. It's not safe to be walking around looking like that."

I nodded, my heart racing. "Let me just see him first, and then I'll get cleaned up. Promise."

The nurse gave me a dubious look, and I followed her to the back. I saw Sawyer standing outside a room, and my knees shook.

"He's okay?"

"He's waiting for you. He's fine. Apparently, he couldn't find his phone, and when he did, he could only get one text out, to the person he texted last, before it died. Crushed, apparently. Give him a break, okay?"

I narrowed my gaze, anger at the situation warring with all the other emotions running through me. I hoped it wasn't pregnancy hormones this early. But wow, I needed to hit something.

"I'll figure it out," I grumbled as I moved through the door.

Gus lay there, slightly bruised, a bandage on his shoulder, and a small smile on his face.

"Hey there, babe. Good to know you're okay."

"You asshole. I can't believe you sacrificed yourself for me."

Gus's eyes widened. "But you're fine, right? Did you get checked out?"

There was a slight ringing in my ears, and my pulse increased. I could hear my heartbeat in my head, but I swallowed and stepped forward.

"I'm fine. Of course, I'm fine. Because nothing hurt me. You took the whole of it. Rather than doing what we trained for."

Gus narrowed his gaze. "I did what I was trained to do. I protected both of us."

"Yet you got hurt."

"But you didn't."

"Gus," I said, but then my tongue felt a little heavy, my eyes droopy.

"Jennifer? Jennifer! Sawyer! Call the nurse. Jen. Jen."

He kept repeating my name. As I fell, I tried to respond to him.

Somehow, Sawyer caught me, and then nurses and doctors were there.

"Damn it. Why didn't you get checked out?" Gus shouted over the med team.

"Ma'am? Ma'am? Can you hear me?" the nurse asked.

"Sorry. I guess my knees went weak from all the adrenaline."

She kept her gaze steady. "When was the last time you ate?"

"This morning."

They asked a few more questions, and I tried my best to answer, but I wasn't tracking well. "Any chance you're pregnant?" she asked, and it was as if she'd thrown a bomb.

I looked past her at Gus, who sat up, wincing as he did. I nodded, looking back at the nurse. "Sorry."

Then my knees went weak and there was nothing.

Chapter 7

Gus

"You really shouldn't be getting up," Sawyer warned, trying to push me back onto the bed. But damn it, I needed to see her face and yell at her for scaring at me. They had wheeled her out of here into the next room, and I could hear her talking, but I needed to see her. Why wouldn't they let me see her?

"Just let me get up. I need to get over there."

"And if you tear a stitch? You really want me to have to face Jen or any of your teammates? Because I might work out, but I don't work for a security company." Sawyer flexed his biceps, and I rolled my eyes. Thankfully, I didn't have a headache or a concussion, though it had been a near thing.

It was all I could do not to remember the explosion. The man coming toward us, all my training out the window. All because I needed to protect Jen.

And apparently our unborn child.

I swallowed at that, trying to come to terms with the ramifications of that information.

I had willingly nearly sacrificed everything for her. And I would do it again in a heartbeat. Because I loved her.

Holy hell. Things had truly just changed. Only I wasn't sure how we were supposed to deal with it all.

I knew I wouldn't be able to deal with it sitting in this room.

"Why are you looking at me like that?" Sawyer asked. "Please, don't do anything stupid."

I shook my head, slowly moving my feet off the bed.

"Give me some pants. I'm not going to show my ass around the hospital."

"If you go and confront her right now, that'll be showing your ass in a different way."

I flipped my brother off. "Please. Pants. I need to see her. I need to make sure she's okay."

Sawyer studied my face for a long moment before nodding.

"I just need to see her, Sawyer. Please."

Sawyer sighed and then went to the bag he had brought with him. "Mom's going to kill me if she finds out I did this."

"Mom's going to kick my ass if I don't actually speak with Jennifer before she finds out."

As soon as I said the words, he turned to me, and both of us widened our eyes. "Shit. Yes. You need to talk with her. Now."

He helped me get dressed quickly, and then I slowly moved to the room beside us.

Daisy stood there, her gaze narrowed. "What the hell are you doing up?"

I held up my hand as Sawyer slowly backed away. Weakling. Though I didn't tell him that. Mostly because I was afraid of Daisy, too.

"Just let me talk to her."

"We need to make sure you are healthy enough to stand up, too, you know."

"I'm fine. A clean bill of health."

She looked pointedly at my bandage, and I shrugged, immediately regretting it. "I'm going to be fine. Nothing permanent. I just need to make sure she's safe. Please."

"They're keeping her for observation. *Fix this*. I want my people to be okay."

I nodded and made my way into the room. Jen sat on the bed, still in her clothes, hooked up to a machine showing her pulse and blood pressure. Everything looked good, and I was grateful for that.

When she met my gaze, my heart just…stopped. Jennifer had always been beautiful to me. Always something more. It was usually hard for me to keep my gaze off her. The way she lit up a room. It was her strength, her beauty, everything about her.

I'd craved her from the moment I saw her and had done my best to be *one of the guys* with her so she wouldn't see. Wouldn't know.

And then I had one moment of ecstasy, a moment that meant everything.

I wanted more. I had been working up the courage to tell her how I felt, to say fuck the complications.

And now it seemed we had an even larger one.

"Why are you out of bed?" she asked, a small smile playing on her face. "What am I saying? Of course, you're not listening to directions. Why *wouldn't* you be walking around after having part of a wall fall on top of you?"

"I needed to be here. To see you in person. You passed out in front of me."

"So did you. Right on top of me, and then everyone pulled you away from me, and I didn't get to see you. I just saw the blood." She paled again, and I cursed, moving to the side of her bed. I wanted to reach out and take her hand. But I didn't.

"I'm fine," I said after a moment, studying her face.

"I'm fine, too."

But what did *fine* mean?

"At least sit down so you don't fall."

"Okay. Okay." I took the seat next to her bed and scooted it forward. When it pulled at my stitches, I winced, and Jennifer cursed under her breath.

"The nurses don't know you're in here, do they? So when they find you've skipped out, they're going to get angry."

"And they'll blame me, not you. I'm really okay."

"You threw yourself on top of me."

"I didn't even think twice. I knew we couldn't stop him in time. I refused to let you get hurt, Jen."

Her eyes clouded. "I'm just so pissed off that *you* got hurt. For me."

I shook my head. "We both could've been hurt worse."

"I know. But I can take care of myself."

"I know you can. That's what I've always liked about you. It's why we work so well together."

When she let out a sigh, I squeezed her hand. "But we haven't been working well together recently. Because you keep trying to step in to protect me."

"I guess I have another reason to now."

"I really didn't want you to find out that way." When she put her hand over her stomach, it felt like everything changed.

I swallowed hard, staring at where her hand rested. "You're pregnant." I whispered the words as if they weren't quite real. "How long have you known?"

I reached down and gripped her hand. None of this made sense. We were doing this the wrong way, but something was shifting. Something happened, and I didn't know how to fix it.

"Three days. Well, four now." She let out a breath. "I didn't know how to tell you. I was going to tell you soon, though. That's why I wanted to talk. But then it sounded like a weird relationship we-need-to-talk thing. And I realized that it really *is* a weird relationship kind of thing. Because I'm pregnant."

My ears rang as I tried to come to terms with what she was saying. It didn't feel real. None of this did.

"I can't believe it."

"Me either. I mean, we used a condom. *And* I'm on birth control." She paused. "Oh, my God. I should go to my doctor because I don't think I can be on birth control while pregnant. I'll need to have it removed. Oh, hell. I have a doctor's appointment scheduled for tomorrow. But I should tell the doctor here."

I squeezed her hand and nodded. "Okay. Okay. Hell. This is a lot."

"I guess the bomb and the wall falling on top of us is only the second most explosive thing to happen today," she said with a laugh before tears filled her eyes.

I moved to wipe the moisture from her cheeks. "Don't cry, Jen, baby. We'll figure this out."

"I don't know what to do."

"I'm not going to let you do it alone. No matter what happens. I'm here."

"But we didn't even want to be together."

I frowned at her. "We said it would be easier if we weren't. But nothing about this is easy, is it?"

She opened her mouth to say something, and I was ready to bare it all, to tell her what I felt, but then the nurses came in, and I was pulled away.

I wanted to stay, I wanted to figure it out. She wasn't mine. And I had to remember that.

Even if I wanted her to be.

* * * *

"I'm fine, Mom. Seriously. Sawyer is on his way over with dinner, and then I'm going to rest."

"You're sure you don't have to work today? I will call your employers. My baby's hurt."

I barely resisted the urge to roll my eyes. My parents were freaking amazing, but they also tended to baby us. How Sawyer and I ended up as accident-prone and daredevil kids, I didn't know.

"Whatever you do, please don't call the Montgomerys. I don't want to be the one with the mommy who calls my boss."

"This mommy will call whoever I need to make sure her baby's okay." She sounded so stern it made me smile.

"I'm going to be fine. You checked on me yourself. Now, you're back at work, and I'm not. Of course, I am off duty for a little bit. But there are just a few stitches. A couple of bumps. That's it. No broken bones. No concussion. I'm fine."

"I didn't like hearing on the news that the building I knew you were in was blown up. I wish you would get a better job. One where you're nice and safe and nothing ever happens."

I sighed at the familiar refrain. "Things happen every day everywhere. I like being in a position where I can help, you know?"

My mom was silent for a while before she finally replied. "I know, I know. And I'm grateful you're in that position, too. Now, let your brother take care of you. And maybe that young woman who was in the room next door. You know, the one you never stop talking about?" There was a question in her voice, and I could practically see the smile on her face, even through the phone.

"Okay, Mom. I'm going to let you go. Thank you, though."

"I will get details out of you, mister. Just you wait."

I said my goodbyes, and we hung up. Oh, she was going to get some details soon. Because Jennifer and I needed to talk. Everything remained unresolved after the nurses kicked me out of her hospital room. Then my parents showed up, and the doctors discharged me. Now, I was home, it had been twenty-four hours since I'd seen her, and I was on a loaner phone until I could get a replacement. I wanted to text her just to see how she was. Ask how the baby was.

I nearly freaked out at that thought. *Baby.* She was pregnant.

I mean, I knew how it happened. I knew when it happened. But it still didn't seem real.

It had been over two months since I'd kissed her, held her. Since we'd let the heat between us burn. Now, everything had changed.

What was I supposed to do with that?

The doorbell rang, and since I didn't have my phone where I could see the camera, I heaved myself up off the couch and made my way to the front of the house. My heart raced when I saw who stood outside.

I opened the door quickly, fumbling with the locks. I watched Jennifer play with her fingers and bite her lip—those luscious lips that I'd tasted, still craved.

"Jen. You're here."

"I could have asked Daisy for your new number, but then she would have asked why, and she kind of already knows. I just want this to be between us for now. Which is probably a lot in retrospect. I thought it was finally time we have that talk." She let out a breath. "And I'm saying a lot of words all at once without really letting you respond. Are you okay? Do you want me to let you be?"

I quickly reached out and grabbed her arm, pulling her to my side. Just the heat of her, the feel of her, did things to me. I was a goner, and I didn't even know when it happened. Was it the first time I saw her? The first time I worked with her?

I closed the door behind her and just stood there, feeling awkward as hell. I wasn't sure what to say, let alone how to feel. But I wanted to feel something. I loved this woman. I had for months, and I hadn't even realized it.

I just needed to figure out exactly what to do with that feeling.

There was no going back now. We were beyond that.

"Can I get you something to drink? Do you need to sit down? Are you feeling okay? What about morning sickness?" I kept asking questions, my voice pitching higher with each one.

She smiled at me and shook her head.

"I'm kind of glad I'm not the only person freaking out right now. Because I'm really freaking out."

"Oh, good. So, we're in the same position. That is good to know."

"None of this is what I expected. I was trying to get over you, and now here we are, doing this." She pressed her lips together, and I felt triumphant. But I figured that probably wasn't the best way to get her to stay still for one minute and talk with me.

"Let's sit down and think. Because it's been a busy few days."

"Tell me about it. Once I'm done here, I get to go into work and have a discussion with the crew and figure out what the hell I'm going to do."

I faltered as we sat, ignoring the twinge in my shoulder. "With work? Or in general?"

She gave me a small smile and swallowed. "That's the thing. I don't want to be out in the field if I'm a liability or could hurt the baby."

A sense of relief hit me so hard, it must have shown on my face.

Because she narrowed her eyes. "I can handle anything, Gus. I can take care of myself. And I know that's something you've had trouble with in the past."

I scowled. "I know you can handle yourself."

"Do you? Because you're constantly pushing me out of the way or trying to take over things to help me. And while I appreciate that somewhat as a partner, I feel like you sometimes forget that I can handle things myself. That I'm trained just as much as you. We've always butted heads like that. And it's not just because I'm a woman. You don't do those things with Daisy."

"Because I don't feel the same things for Daisy."

She stopped, and I realized I might've actually said the right thing this time. "I want you, Jen. I've wanted you for a hell of a long time. It took me way too fucking long to realize that, to get the words out. But I do. I want you. And the only reason I stayed back, the only reason I wouldn't let myself say how I felt for as long as I did was because I respected you. I respected who we were at work. We thought it was too complicated for us to be together while working. But the problem is, I don't want to wait anymore. I want you, Jennifer. I want to figure this out. Ford and Noah can figure it out, why can't we?"

"Ford and Noah are the bosses. They make the rules."

"And both of them told me flat-out that we could be together."

She whirled on me before standing and beginning to pace.

"You talked to them about this?"

"I didn't tell them anything, not that we've been together, and especially not about the baby. But I assume Daisy knows."

"I made the same hand movement that I did to you. She put two and two together. I don't know if the guys know, but they will as soon as I have that meeting. But first I need to figure out what the hell I'm doing."

"Okay, then let's figure out what the hell *we're* doing."

"We?"

"Of course, we. I want you, Jennifer. We could make sure we don't work side by side if it's a problem. Then I wouldn't have to choose between you and the client because I wouldn't be beside you. Though it will kill me not to be able to protect you."

"Again, I only need you as my partner when we're on a job. I don't need you to protect me."

"But I want to. Just like I want you to protect me. That's what partners do."

"But it gets complicated when you add feelings into it."

"We're not automatons. Of course, there's going to be feelings."

"Then we need to make decisions past that. Figure out what those feelings mean."

"I'm sitting here. Looking at you. No—wanting you."

"And this baby? It changes everything."

"You're right, it does." I stood up and faced her. When I pushed her hair back from her face, she sucked in a breath.

"Gus, I'm worried."

"About what?"

"This is already going to change everything. I don't want to lose you as my friend."

"We're having a baby, Jennifer. I think everything's going to change no matter what. But I want you. I want to be *with* you. Let me be with you. Let me show you that, yes, the complications are hard, but we can make it work."

"Okay."

I stood there, blinking as I tried to absorb exactly what she'd said.

"Did you just say okay?"

She burst out laughing and took a step back. I slid my hand down her shoulder, taking her fingers and squeezing.

"Yes. Okay. Do you realize how hard it's been this past year wanting you and not being able to do anything about it? I thought we were just friends."

"We are friends. And maybe that's the problem."

"True. We have this chemistry and connection, and I want to see what happens. But I don't want to screw everything up at work. And the fact that—oh, my God, we're going to be parents. This doesn't even seem real."

"It doesn't feel real." I paused. "Did you make an appointment with your doctor?"

"Tomorrow morning." She bit her lip. "Do you want to go? I mean, everything's up in the air and I don't know what we are or what this is, but—"

I didn't even let her finish the statement. I took her face in my hands and pressed my mouth to hers, cutting her off. She tasted of sugar and spice. She moaned against me, and I wrapped my arms around her, ignoring the pain in my shoulder from my stitches.

I'd craved her from the moment I saw her, and this felt like a promise.

I didn't want to stop.

When I finally pulled away and pressed my forehead to hers, I let out a shaky breath.

"Okay."

"We're going to do this backward."

"What do you mean by *this*?" she asked, humor in her eyes.

I threw my head back and laughed as I held her.

"Maybe that, too. First though, I want you. I want to be here. I want to figure out what the hell we're doing. At work, with this baby, everything. So, I want to take you out on a damn date."

"I guess we sort of skipped that."

"We're friends, and I've wanted you forever."

"Same."

"Then let me show you what I feel for you. Let me prove to you I can do this."

"Okay. So, tomorrow. Baby's first appointment."

I paled. "Holy hell, it's real."

"It is. I guess we should make sure we don't screw it up."

I pushed her hair from her face and leaned down, taking her lips with mine again.

"We're not going to screw it up. We're going to overthink it, we're going to make it complicated, but we're going to make it real. I promise. I'm going to be there for you, Jennifer. As your partner."

"Just not on the job."

I kissed her again, ignoring the ache in my heart because we made good partners. We were the best. But if that's what it took, I would step back. I would work with others.

I needed her to trust me.

I needed her to love me.

Just as much as I loved her.

Chapter 8

Jennifer

My stomach roiled. I wasn't sure if it was the morning sickness that had become my worst enemy, or nerves about the meeting coming up.

I was supposed to meet with the team right after Gus, but there hadn't been a chance. The company we worked with—the one that'd set us up for failure—had an emergency, and Noah and Ford needed to be there. So, I figured I'd at least meet with Daisy to go over my options.

It had been three days since Gus had kissed me again and said he wanted to be my partner.

We hadn't defined what that meant.

I knew it was more than just working beside me, which was something we still had to deal with. But I didn't know how to process what I felt for him.

Honestly, I had never let myself feel much for him beyond what I had already revealed. When the attack happened, I'd told myself I loved him, but now, my brain and heart weren't agreeing. I *couldn't* love him.

If I'd let myself love him, it could all have been ruined.

Now here we were, about to face an uncertain future together. So, perhaps I should figure things out and let myself love him.

That was such a scary thing. I didn't feel ready.

Did it matter? Not when we had a chance. A possible future.

First things first. I needed to figure out how to do the job I loved and still remain a large part of the team—a helpful member of the team, But I couldn't risk everything because it wasn't just me anymore. It was this baby. And it was Gus.

I had been slowly falling for him all along. Or perhaps it wasn't slow at all. After all, I had been doing my best not to think about him like that for a very long time. Perhaps all of that was coming to fruition much faster than I'd planned.

I made my way to the coffee shop first. Latte on the Rocks was owned by friends of mine.

The whole building was owned by the Montgomerys, and I loved that they were creating a community with their huge family. There was the coffee shop and bakery owned by Greer and Raven—both of them Montgomerys themselves. On the other side of them was a gallery and art studio—not just for Montgomerys, although the Montgomery family had a lot of artists, as well. I didn't go in there often. Usually because I was working too hard.

"You doing okay?"

I looked up to see Raven standing there, a small smile on her face. "You look a bit worried."

"Oh, just thinking."

"About Gus? I saw him earlier today with the guys as they were heading out. I can't believe he's already back on duty."

I rolled my eyes as I followed Raven into the coffee shop.

"He's on partial duty. He's not going out on bodyguard assignments, just installations. He's not even allowed to do recon."

"That's good. Because it would stress me out if anything else happened. I don't know how you do it."

I frowned as I made my way to the front counter.

"How I do what? My job?"

"You kick ass, you're trained, and you know what you're doing. I meant letting someone you care about do it. Of course, all my friends seem to be in that position these days."

"How did you…what did you…what?"

Raven winced as she waved at a regular.

"I'm sorry. Are you and Gus not together? Am I just seeing things?"

I tried to find an answer to that because it wasn't as clear as it should be.

"Oh. We're not. Well, maybe. We're just taking it slow."

So slow that I was pregnant with his child. But we weren't ready to tell people that.

"Well, that's great. You guys just always seem so in tune. I assumed. Plus, he talks about you all the time. And he always knows your order. Even though you don't have a regular order. I love it."

I blushed. "He's great at that, isn't he?"

"He is. He's a good guy. I'm glad he's okay."

"I'm really glad he's okay, too."

"You guys do such a great job, and I'm grateful for it. Especially when I needed help." Raven swallowed hard, and I reached out and squeezed her hand. She had been through hell, but we'd found the guy.

I still didn't like to think about that. I didn't like it when my friends were in danger.

"Anyway," she said with a bright smile that reached her eyes, "I guess that's what happens when you have someone to rely on. Someone you love with everything you are. And now I'm getting personal. I'm sorry."

I shook my head. "No, it's okay. I guess most people thought we were together."

"Part of me wants to know if you are now. But again, I'm just your baker, nothing more."

"I'd like to think you're my friend after all these months of me eating every single baked good you make."

I rubbed my hand over my stomach, the scent of lemon hitting me. I staggered a bit, shaking my head. "I was going to ask for a lemon bar, but maybe not."

Raven studied my face before her eyes widened. "Oh. Oh!"

"Please, don't say anything," I mumbled quickly, hands outstretched.

"I won't. Well. I'm just going to take all my secrets and burning questions and walk over here. Let me get you some tea. Does that sound good? Maybe with some oat milk?"

"That sounds amazing."

"We've got you. And it's decaf, too."

Well, that just confirmed she knew I was pregnant. I would have to be better about hiding it. I was still in the first trimester. I didn't want everybody to know yet. I hadn't told my family. We hadn't told his. I didn't know which of our friends knew, and keeping my facial expressions a little more passive. But first, I needed to come to terms with this myself before the rest of the world knew.

I spoke to Raven for a bit longer before grabbing my things and heading over to the security building past the tattoo shop. Montgomery Ink Legacy was going strong, and I could see Raven's man, Sebastian, working on a back piece through the window. I waved at Lake, who was one of the owners, and she smiled back. Everybody was just so happy, finding their ways and their paths.

I was sort of stumbling. And it was working, but what if it quit? What if I realized I had no idea what I was doing?

I couldn't help but think back to just a few days prior when I was sitting there listening to my doctor as she explained everything.

Gus had been there, the two of us sitting wide-eyed as we looked at the dot on an ultrasound that didn't even look the size of a grain of rice.

But it was. We were having a baby. And we were starting something new. A new relationship.

It didn't feel real. It needed to. Because reality was a cold shock of water to the system, and there was no going back.

He'd held my hand as we listened, as we tried to come to terms with exactly what was happening. Because it *was* happening.

I wanted this baby. A smile spread over my face as I walked into the office, realizing that was the truth. I wanted this child. And I wanted it with Gus.

"Hey there," Kate said, pulling me out of my life-altering revelations.

I looked up at her and smiled. "Hey. I didn't know you were in today."

"I'm trying to be in most days. Even just for a minute. I wanted to get a few things done."

"You're doing a great job, Kate. I really appreciate it."

"That's sweet of you to say. Thank you. I'm trying my best. And I love working with you guys."

"Seriously. You keep us up to date, and you make sure we're organized. We need that. It might sound weird to say, but lives depend on it."

Kate blew out a breath. "That's frightening but thank you. You know, I always thought it would be a little scary to work in the security business. But it's fun. You guys are a big family."

I nodded, my smile stretching. "We are. Even if we fight sometimes."

"Well true. The fighting is fun, though. And you're right next to some very hot tattoo artists. Although I'm pretty sure all of them are taken by now. Just my luck."

I laughed, sitting down at my seat.

"Have a thing for tattoo artists?"

She waved a hand in front of her face. "Don't you know it. I don't know, it's just the ink."

"Plenty of men have ink without being tattoo artists."

"I'm pretty sure all the guys who work here do. It helps that they're the tattoo artists' cousins."

"That is true. Gus has ink, too."

Kate winked at me. "None showing, So, how do you know that?"

"I'm not answering any questions, missy."

Kate laughed. "If that was too forward, let me know. However, he's hot."

"Who's hot?" Daisy asked as she walked through the front door.

"No one," I said quickly as Kate blurted, "Gus."

"Oh. He's okay."

"Okay, those are fighting words," I said with a laugh.

"And if I said he was hot, would you fight me for him?"

"I will never fight another woman over a man. That just seems like a waste of resources."

"It is a waste of resources. We could take over the world if we weren't waiting for guys to notice us."

"Excuse me, guys notice you."

Daisy rolled her eyes. "Oh, sure they do. And then they realize I own a business and don't want to sleep with them so they can *protect the little lady*, and can probably kick their asses, too. Then they suddenly have egos they can't contain." She rolled her eyes. "And then they start discussing the size of their egos and how theirs are bigger than the guys I work with, even though ninety percent of the men I work with are related to me."

"I have a feeling that ego in this case means penis," Kate said, not so quietly.

I nodded sagely. "You know what, I do believe you cracked her code."

"Seriously, though. They get so worried that I'm working with guys who could break them with their pinkies that they forget I'm not only related to those guys—minus Gus, of course, and any of the contract workers—but that I could also probably break them with *my* pinky. Not that I would. I don't actually like violence. Anyway, dating is hard, and I hate it. And I'm never doing it again."

"You should do it again. You just need to find a guy who understands."

Daisy looked like she was about to say something, then shook her head.

"I don't know. Anyway, let's go over the checklist," she said, and I stood up, my stomach roiling again.

"Let's do it."

Kate looked worried for a moment but didn't ask questions. I was glad for that. We went to the back office—the secure one, where nobody could listen in. I was grateful for that because I wasn't sure what was about to happen.

"Are the guys going to be here?"

"No, it's just you and me." Daisy smiled. "We're friends. Yes, I'm your boss, and yes, my cousins own the company with me, but we're not firing you. I promise. We're just going to go over what you want to do because our job can be dangerous. I want you to be able to work and not feel that you need to put yourself in any situations that will be too much. I'm not going to tell you what *too much* is because that is up to you. I promise."

For some reason, tears stung my eyes. I wiped my face.

"I know that. I knew that. I don't know, I was just really worried about sitting in here in front of a bunch of men, men who happen to be my friends, but I didn't want to have to explain my body to them."

"You're not explaining your body to me, let alone being in a room alone with dudes. No, what's going to happen right now is you will tell me what you want. Or nothing. Just talk, Jen. You're the one who wanted this meeting."

I sighed and rubbed my temples. "I'm pregnant."

Daisy smiled at me, her face going soft. "I know."

"I haven't really said it out loud too many times. I'm pregnant. I'm having a baby. With Gus."

"Why do you sound so incredulous about that last part?" Daisy asked with a laugh.

"Because we only had sex one time."

I wasn't about to tell her where.

"Wow. Should I tell him he has strong swimmers and you have a very strong uterus?"

"Dear God."

"I know. This just went way past weird into *what the hell*. Seriously, though, congratulations." She paused. "Is it a congratulations? I never know what to say. Usually, people who tell me they're pregnant have been trying, at least in my small circle of friends."

"I think I'm happy." I sighed and sipped my tea. "I always wanted to be a mom. To find the perfect man and get married and have a baby. In that order," I said sarcastically.

"Well, you found Gus. I guess that counts as some form of order."

"Only we haven't even been on a date."

Daisy's eyes widened, but she didn't ask any questions.

"We're figuring things out. We haven't given any declarations, and it's way too early for that I think, but we're friends. And we're partners. And now we're going to be partners in a different sense. We're going on a date tomorrow."

Daisy grinned. "See? That works."

"I hope so. I hope we don't screw everything up at work or anything. But speaking of work, I want to make sure I don't partner with him. Would that be weird? Gus and I discussed it. At first, I thought I wanted it because he keeps putting himself in the line of fire for me, but then again, I want to do the same for him. But it's not just me anymore."

Daisy nodded. "Ford and Noah are only on the same assignments when we have a large group. They don't go out together anymore. So, no, you two won't be assigned to the same cases. It'll help keep some separation for home-life versus work-life, as well. But you guys are professionals, and I trust you. Now, do you want to be out in the field?"

I shook my head. "No. I want to do installations, and I want to work in the office. I'll do training, and I can help any of the recruits we have coming in. But I don't want to be in a situation where I feel like I could have gotten me or my baby killed again."

"No pipe bombs with walls falling on top of you?" Daisy said dryly.

"And no warehouses that explode when you take a step in," I said cautiously.

Daisy's eyes tightened, but she nodded.

Daisy still hadn't talked about the attack. She needed to. She was my friend, and I would force her into it soon.

"So, we'll make it work. You're amazing at what you do. And the thing with this business is that we're not out there playing James Bond. We're keeping people safe, but we also work on installs and surveillance for new buildings and companies. Hell, the Cage brothers own enough companies and businesses out there to keep us in the black for the rest of our lives. You could just work on those installs and still not get them all done in your lifetime."

"That's good to know," I said with a laugh.

"Right? If you think the Montgomerys are taking over the world, you haven't met the Cages yet."

"That's one thing down. Now to figure out the rest."

"I know I was out there saying I'm never going to find a man and everything's hard because they don't see me, but Gus sees you. He sees all of us. We're very lucky with the guys we work with. It just sucks that most happen to be related to me."

I smirked as we stood up and made our way out to Kate.

"We'll find you someone."

"Maybe. Or maybe I'll be the spinster aunt."

Kate cleared her throat. "Actually, I think you might be too old to be a spinster now. There's an age limit on that."

"You know, I was just starting to like you, Kate."

"Oh, I love you, too."

The door opened, and I looked up, expecting to see a client or maybe even Gus, but I froze, recognizing the man.

"Mr. Davis, what can I do for you?"

Davis, as in the man who'd hired us for our ill-fated job. The one who'd lied to us. Who'd put in motion the actions that had nearly gotten me and Gus killed.

That Mr. Davis.

The same Mr. Davis who now held a gun on us, sweat beading on his brow, and a snarl on his face.

"You've ruined me, you stupid bitch. You ruined me."

And then he fired.

Chapter 9

Gus

"So, you're quitting on us now after you decided to play chicken with a wall and failed?" Kane asked, and I flipped him off.

"Aren't you the one who fell out of a moving car?"

On the other side of Kane, Kingston snorted, shaking his head.

"I did not fall out of a car. I was getting out of the vehicle when Noah decided to move forward without telling me. I was fine. I didn't fall out."

"No, you sort of tumbled into a roll." Kane ducked his cousin's fist.

"You guys are ridiculous."

"Maybe. But we're your favorites."

"So, are you staying?"

"Of course, I'm staying. I love this job. And I can somewhat handle you guys."

Kane just rolled his eyes. "Thanks. We try, Gus-Gus."

"Please, don't call me that. You know how long it took me to get rid of that nickname after elementary school?"

"At least I'm not the kid who was named after a mouse from Cinderella," Kingston said.

I flipped them both off. "I can't believe I drunkenly told you that. My mom loved that fat little mouse."

"Well, that fat little mouse helped save the day." Kane nodded sagely as he said it.

"You know, I have a cousin named Gus, too," Kingston added.

"You have a cousin named everything. There are no more names out there when it comes to Montgomerys. You have taken them all."

"That is true. Have you met Gus? Is it a Gus-ception if you guys do meet?" Kane laughed at his joke, while Kingston and I just shook our heads.

"I might have met him. It's Sebastian's brother, right?"

"Yep. So, technically not either of our cousins. We're second cousins with him."

"Please don't make me do your family tree. I don't have it in me. I will throw something," I said, not quite joking.

"It's true. He will throw something. And it will be all your fault," Kingston added.

"So, you and Jen?" Kane put in, and Kingston led out an audible groan.

"Oh, God. Are you just asking all the tough questions without thinking about the consequences? Come on, man. You don't want this guy to kick your ass. Because he could."

"That's so true. And I can."

"No, you can't. We all know I'm the stronger one."

Kingston and I snorted at the same time.

"No, I could totally take you!"

"We are in the parking lot of our building," Kane said as he held up his hands.

"Are you not entertained?"

"How many times have you seen that movie?" I asked.

"Enough I can quote it word for word. Come on, Gus-Gus. Let's see how you roll with those stitches."

"If you pop one, it won't only be Jen that kicks your ass. Daisy will, too. Hell, all of us will kick your ass."

"He's not going to pop a stitch because I can take him."

"What is up your ass right now?" I asked, and Kane just shook his head.

"I'm fine."

"I'm going with women problems," I said softly toward Kingston, who nodded.

"Huge women problems. Big-time women problems. So, who is she, and what the fuck did you do to ruin it?" Kingston asked.

Kane sighed and waved his arms between us. "It's not women problems."

"Well, then, why are you asking about Jen? Trying to put the attention on me rather than anything having to do with you? I see how it is."

"I'm not. I promise. I was just wondering. We like Jen. We like the two of you together. You two have been tiptoeing around each other for a fucking year. I thought once you two slept together, things would be different, but no, you just got weirder." I froze, looking at Kane and then at Kingston.

"Excuse me? How do you know we slept together?"

"Well, the way you acted around each other was different. Still scorching chemistry, but like it was soothed a bit because you got it out of your systems," Kane replied.

"Plus, you didn't delete all the backup tapes," Kingston said with a wince.

The blood drained out of my face before I put my hands on my temples and rubbed. "Please, tell me you deleted that. And no one actually saw... You didn't show everyone... Because I'm going to have to kill you, and then I'll go to jail, and it'll be a whole thing. I really don't have it in me to go to jail for killing you."

Kingston cleared his throat. "It was my turn to go through the logs, I only saw the kissing and the shirt pulling. Then I deleted as much of it as I could."

"What do you mean by that? As much of it as you could."

Kingston winced again. "I deleted a chunk of time before and after. When Noah and Ford do the audit, I'll deal with it."

"So, no one saw anything, and you didn't watch?"

"Of course, not. You know I love Jen, she's like a sister. So much like a sister that I really didn't want to see her having sex. I don't want to see my friends having sex, voyeurism is not my kink. And no, I'm not talking about my kinks," he blurted before anyone could ask.

"Anyway," he said, trying to change the subject. "I also don't need to see your hairy ass."

"Excuse me, my ass is not hairy. It is pristine. And I can out-squat all of you."

"Please tell me we're not going to have a squat-off." Kane pinched the bridge of his nose. "Of course. Now, I just want to say squat-off again because it's so fucking ridiculous."

"Thank you for deleting it," I said, my tone low.

"No problem. And, seriously, I'll deal with Ford and Noah."

"Why?"

Kingston ran his hands over his face. "Because I've already had to delete video from them. It has apparently become my role in this company to delete the office porn from the security tapes. We're going to need to have a lovely seminar about having sex in the building. Because, my God, if I have to see one more hairy ass—"

"My ass isn't hairy!"

"If I have to see one more *hairy ass*," Kingston continued, "I'm going to strangle someone. Or I'm just going to whack off on camera and force everyone to watch it. You know, make my own porn. I'd be good at it."

"I'd be better," Kane joked, and I just rolled my eyes.

"You guys are ridiculous."

"We really are. But don't worry. Your privacy is safe. And I didn't see anything. Not even your hairy ass."

"Stop talking about my ass. And it's not hairy."

"Speaking of hairy situations." Kane winked. "See what I did there?"

"Not even a little subtle," Kingston mumbled.

"You and Jen? Are you together? Are you not? Tell us. Give us all the details."

"Would you like me to braid your hair as I do?"

He brushed his hand through his long locks. "It is getting to the point where you could braid it. Maybe one day."

"I don't know. We're partners. We're figuring things out. But well…fuck." I let out a breath. "I love her."

Both men stopped joking around and stared at me.

"You love her? Really?" Kingston asked.

"Really. I don't know when it happened, it just did. And I don't know what we're supposed to do about it. But I love her. So now, here I am, trying to make sure I don't screw everything up by being who I am."

"What do you mean by that?" Kane asked.

"By being demanding or overprotective. By letting my instincts rule and throwing myself into every situation to protect her. This job is dangerous. And I love her. Fuck. I love her. I'm in love with Jen."

"I don't know if you should say that any louder because then everybody in our family who happens to be in this building will hear you," Kingston said quickly.

I sighed as I rubbed my temple. "I don't know what to do about it. But I'm going to figure it out. We're going on a date."

"You put the cart before the horse. Nice."

"Well, since you love her, and you've already slept together, I suppose a date would be helpful," Kane put in.

"I can't believe I'm getting advice from a man who has never actually had a real girlfriend." I fist-bumped Kingston, but Kane just looked at us and shook his head.

It seemed I'd hit the target—the secret he didn't want to tell. But I wasn't going to push.

Since I was keeping a big secret. A huge fucking one.

I was going to be a father.

That didn't even seem real.

It was unexpected, but I couldn't call it an accident. Not when it was the most beautiful fucking thing ever.

And it was with my best friend. The person I trusted more than anything.

My partner.

And we weren't just a hope. Weren't just a maybe. We could be something far more.

I just had to convince her of that.

"There's something going on behind those eyes of yours. Some a-ha moment. Talk to us," Kingston ordered.

"I need to get her to fall in love with me. I love her and don't want to lose her because I'm too chickenshit to do anything about it."

The two cousins looked at each other and then back at me. "You can't force someone to love you," Kane started, and the way he said it made me worried. What the hell was going on with him? But I knew he wouldn't tell us. He didn't seem ready.

"Just be yourself. Take her out."

"Come on, let's go get some coffee, then we'll head into the office."

I looked at Kingston and nodded. "What do I say to her? What do I do?"

"You be who you are," Kingston said with a shrug. "You should be talking to Noah or Ford, anyone who actually knows what to do in a relationship. But if you want to be with her? Then prove you're worthy of her. Because Jen is one amazing woman. And hell, Gus, you're a great guy, too," he said, and I laughed.

"You two have always worked well together. You guys just click. So, trust the process. Don't chickenshit out of it. Do something about it."

I nodded, knowing he was right. And we were doing this all backward. I would find a way for her to love me. To show her it could work. That I could be the guy for her. And along the way, we'd figure out how to be parents.

We would follow a path—one a little curvier than I ever expected.

I put my hand on the door of the coffee shop, but the sound of a gunshot stopped me in my tracks.

People screamed and ran, but I was moving right alongside Kane and Kingston. We knew where the sound had come from.

I ducked into the gap between the tattoo shop and the security office as Kingston and Kane took cover on the other side of the pillars because the man's back was to us for now.

I gestured toward them, and they nodded. We looked at the door where Mr. Davis stood with a gun in his hand. My thoughts froze.

Because Jen was in there.

I didn't know who else, but I saw her car.

Jen was in there.

With a man who had a gun we just heard fire.

Part of me wanted to move, to take him out, but I didn't know anything about the situation. I didn't know who else was in there and could put everyone in danger.

But the part of me that wanted to keep Jen safe, to keep our child safe, was telling me to ignore my training.

And that was the part Jen hated.

So, I pushed it down and looked toward Kingston. He had his phone out and was looking at the security feed. I froze, my blood turning to ice.

Because Kate, Daisy, and Jennifer were all in there, standing in front of a man with a gun, and there was nothing I could do about it.

Chapter 10

Jennifer

I pulled Kate down as soon as the shot sounded, moving quickly.

She lay under me, shaking and wide-eyed. She hadn't signed up for this. She was an admin, and damn it, I was so pissed off. Here I was, trying to do what was best for my child and my team, and the danger came right into the building.

"Mr. Davis. Please, put the gun down."

He pointed it directly at Daisy as he wiped the back of his other hand across his forehead.

"You don't understand. I worked so hard for this business. I put my life into it. And now it's all gone up in smoke. Literally. The damn man blew up the building. All my investors are backing out. My followers don't want to deal with me anymore because, apparently, I'm too dangerous. If you would've just listened. If you had understood, this wouldn't have happened. I would still be making money. But instead, I'll have to beg on the street."

I highly doubted that was the case. He was being investigated for criminal activities thanks to what the authorities had found, but that wasn't on us. We had nothing to do with it.

But here he was, putting us in danger.

I slowly sat up, blocking Kate. He didn't seem to mind me moving, so I continued to stand, nodding at Daisy. Someone must have heard the shot, and though we hadn't been able to send out an alert, the security system would. Whoever was outside would, as well. The authorities were probably already on their way, and our team would be here soon.

We needed to contain this before it got too dangerous.

"I'm just so tired. So tired of all of this."

"I understand," I said as he moved toward Daisy.

Daisy looked like she wanted to curse at me, but I wasn't about to let him shoot again. He had shot into the ceiling, and who knew what would happen if he got off another round. It could go into the wall, hit someone in the tattoo shop, or someone outside. Or anyone in here.

"It wasn't fair that man took his frustrations out on you. But you don't need to do the same here. You can just put the gun down, and we'll talk it over. But we can't talk to you when you have a gun pointed at us. Don't you see that we're scared?"

Kate let out a whimpering sound. I wasn't sure if it was real or not, but he seemed to understand and wavered just a bit.

"I don't want to hurt anyone. I just want things to go back to the way they were."

"Then let's talk it over. But we can't do that with a gun in your hand."

"I'm just so tired."

When he lowered the gun, Daisy and I moved. She had the weapon out of his hand immediately, and I got him on the ground, my knee in his back, his arms behind him before he could even call out. Kate was on her feet then, phone in hand as she dialed the authorities, and I was so damn proud of how quickly she reacted.

The man under me began to cry.

I wasn't surprised when the back door burst open and Kingston, Kane, and Gus ran through.

"Jennifer!" Gus shouted as he came in.

I saw the fear in his gaze as he took in the situation.

"It's fine. We're fine. If someone could get me some zip ties, that would be great."

"I just want it to stop," Mr. Davis continued to cry, shaking under me.

"I hear sirens. I'll go head them off and make sure they know the situation is handled."

"I'm on the phone with dispatch right now. They understand what they're walking into," Kate said, and another moment of pride slid in.

"Let me handle this?" Kane asked, and I raised a brow.

"Because I can't?"

"No, because I think you should go hug Gus right now."

I met his gaze. I didn't see worry for me there, other than the normal concern for a teammate being in danger. He didn't know I was pregnant. But Gus did. Daisy did. And I did.

"Okay," I said after a moment and then traded places with Kane, letting Gus take my hand to help me up. I could have gotten up myself, but based on the look on his face, he needed to do that. Needed to help.

So, I let him.

The adrenaline began to wear off, and I got nauseous again.

Before I could say anything, to figure out if he was angry that I had taken a risk, or proud because his teammates had taken care of themselves and the situation, the authorities came in. We all stood at attention, hands up so they knew we weren't the threats.

"Tell us what happened," the cop said as he walked in. Daisy began, with Kate and me adding in details.

Kingston handed over the security files, as well as any others we had from the bombing. After two hours of going through everything, they finally left us alone in the now-empty tattoo shop next door.

The security office would be closed for a couple of days. The authorities needed to look it over again, and Noah and Ford wanted to double-check that everything was safe, considering a gun had gone off inside.

There was a bullet hole in the ceiling, and that thought brought chills, though I did my best not to think about it.

"Are you okay?" Gus asked, and I nodded, worried what he might say next.

"I'm fine. Promise. He didn't hurt me."

He kept looking at me as if straining to find a bruise or bullet wound. As if I couldn't take care of myself.

Anger swamped me because I was good at my job. Yes, we had been in danger, but nobody got hurt.

"I'm fine," I snapped. "I can protect myself. I've always been able to. I promise. Even after all these changes, I can still do that."

He narrowed his eyes at me as everybody quieted around us. At this point, I didn't even care that all my team members could hear me and were watching this unfold. If Gus and I were going to make this work, then we'd have to figure it out now.

"I was worried. So fucking worried," Gus growled.

I threw my hands up in the air. "That's fine. But stop looking at me like I'm going to keel over. This isn't going to work between us if you're afraid of me being in danger every moment."

"You were *just* in danger. There was a literal gun in your face."

"Yes, and it was scary, but we handled it." I let out a breath. "I can save myself. You don't need to risk everything to protect me all the time."

"I know that," he gritted out. "I didn't run in to save you, did I? We were formulating a plan when you and Daisy took care of it. I would've been in there if you needed me, but you didn't."

I tried to sense if there was any hurt in him, anything hiding below the words, but I couldn't. "Are you okay with that? That I didn't need you?" I asked softly, afraid of the answer.

"Of course, I'm fine with it. Our jobs are dangerous, Jen."

"I know. And I know I'm going to work in the office for a little while." We were walking a dangerous line with this conversation, but there would be no hiding this pregnancy soon enough. "But, as we just found out, the office isn't always safe. So, we'll have to figure things out, okay?"

"Jen," he whispered, then took a step forward, brushing my hair back from my face. "I want both of us to be safe. All of us," he said, emphasizing the word *all*.

"I'm scared. I was scared. But I'm really afraid that you and I are going to screw this up because you don't trust that I can handle myself."

"You're an idiot," he grumbled. I blinked at him as one of the guys whistled.

"Wrong move," Noah grumbled.

"Excuse me?" I asked, my voice strained.

"We've gone over this already. Of course, I trust you. But I'm sorry if seeing a gun being waved in the face of the woman I love stressed me out. That would've stressed me out even if you were a superhero who could dodge bullets."

My lips twitched. "That would be a scene, wouldn't it?"

"Pretty much. You kicked ass, and while that was scary as hell, I'm not going to forget our plan and how much I love you just because danger keeps trying to find us. But we're going to figure this out. And I keep saying I love you, and you aren't reacting. So, will you please react?"

There was an echo in my ear, like people were talking, and then there was only silence. I tried to figure out what he had just said and what it meant. Because it couldn't be real. This feeling I had inside, this warmth, it couldn't be real.

"You love me?" I asked, my voice barely above a whisper.

"Of course, I do. I know it might seem too soon, but I think I fell in love with you the first week we met, when you kicked my ass, had me down on the mat, and then didn't mock me. You just taught me how to do it better next time. That's when I fell in love with you."

I didn't realize I was crying until he slid his thumbs across my cheeks, wiping away my tears.

"You don't have to love me back yet. But know I'm going to spend the rest of my days making sure you find a way to. I know we have a lot coming up, so many changes, but what I feel? That's not going to change. It might grow a bit, it might settle, might bloom or whatever the hell you want to call it. But I'll always love you."

"And now I'm crying," Kane grumbled, then let out an oof as Daisy elbowed him in the gut.

"Oh."

"Don't say anything," Gus whispered, but then I took his hand in mine.

"I was trying to figure out what this feeling was, this need to always be with you and want you in my life. I thought it was just the intense friendship, our chemistry, but I was wrong."

For some reason, he looked crestfallen. "It's love. I love you so damn much. So please, love me back. Always love me. And let me figure out what the hell we're doing. Because things are about to change and blow up in new and interesting ways. And I can't wait to figure them out with you. There are no maybes about it. I love you, too." Then his lips were on mine, and I was breathing him in, holding him.

All our friends shouted and clapped, whistling their congratulations. I just held on to Gus.

I hadn't recognized what the feeling was.

It had been love all along, the tricky bastard.

But I was really glad I would be with a man who understood it and could figure things out with me.

And be my partner no matter what.

Epilogue

Gus

I slid my hand over her hip, fingers digging into flesh. "I want you."

"Then take me." She purred the words, sliding her ass against my cock. We lay on the bed on our sides, her back to my front.

It was a damn good way to wake up in the morning. I slid my hands over her body, cupping her breasts, swollen and large, overfilling my palms. She had so many new curves, and the way she moved had changed.

I loved my wife, my beautiful, beautiful partner. And now she was all mine, nearly sated and glowing.

She reached around and squeezed my cock. I groaned, closing my eyes.

"Dear God, woman," I growled in her ear.

"Get inside me already. You've been keeping me on the edge for over an hour now and I'm done with it."

"So impatient."

"Of course, I'm impatient. I'm always impatient for you."

I laughed and gently cupped her breasts, playing with her nipples some more. "So sensitive," Jen whispered and then stiffened, her back arching.

"Too sensitive?" I asked, immediately lightening my touch.

She shook her head against me and sighed. "No. Just right. I need you, Gus. Please?"

Her voice sounded so soft and sweet, and I knew she would probably growl at me at any moment. I loved this woman and her mood swings.

Not that I ever called them that. Because if I did, she would break me, and I would let her.

I fucking loved her.

I slid my hands down her again and lifted her thigh, angling myself behind her.

"I love you," I whispered before kissing her shoulder and slowly sinking deep.

She shuddered, her pussy hot, wet, and clamping around my cock.

It was hard to breathe when she was so close, so warm and inviting. I took my time, sliding in and out of her inch by inch until I was finally fully seated, and we were both sweating.

"You are torturing me."

"The best kind of torture, wife." I kissed her shoulder again before moving in slow, lazy strokes.

Our courtship had been a whirlwind. And that was just the tip of the iceberg. Somehow, we'd made a bet and argued into getting married within three months.

I wasn't quite sure how it'd happened, but one day I was holding my girlfriend, my partner, and the next…we were standing in my parents' backyard, my arms around her, my brother at my side, her younger sister at hers, and were vowing to each other that we would take over the world together.

Perhaps not in those terms exactly, but close enough.

Our friends surrounded us, people of our past and hopefully our future.

Nobody seemed surprised that we'd gotten married so fast. I think the world assumed we had been together for over a year, the long months when we had been side by side, pretending we didn't want each other when we truly did.

The way we met, fell in love, and started our family might not be how everybody else would think love happened, but we were in it for the long haul.

Finally, Jen came, clamping around my cock as she moaned, her body flushing beautifully. I followed, having held myself back because I wanted to see her come. Just sinking deep inside her these days could set me off, and that was a problem. But it didn't matter, I needed her.

As we lay there, sweat-slick, I held my wife and willed myself to stay awake.

"We're going to be late for work," she mumbled into the pillow. I sighed before slowly sliding out of her. The sensation nearly sent me over the edge, and from the groan that fell from Jen's mouth, she felt it, too.

"Let's go shower."

"Separately." She huffed out a laugh. "Because we really do need to get to work. You have a meeting, and I have paperwork."

"Yay, paperwork," I teased.

She sat up and flipped me off before sliding her hands over her massive stomach.

I would never call it massive. But she was round with child and looked like some gorgeous goddess of fertility. Again, I wouldn't say that to her. She could kill me with her pinky.

I helped her off the bed because I wanted to, not because she needed me. We had found a balance in that and how we protected each other. I mostly worked with Kane and Kingston these days while she was in the office working with Noah, backing up the cybersecurity branch. She wasn't doing installs as much anymore because standing on a ladder when she was so top-heavy wasn't smart.

As for what would happen after the delivery, our company was connected to a childcare group. Because the Montgomery generation before had so many children, they'd created a daycare so people could still work but have a family member or loved one taking care of their kids. I was grateful that extended to anyone who worked with the Montgomerys. While there weren't as many children as there had been in the previous generation, I had a feeling the Montgomerys and their ilk were only getting started.

We each showered, made our breakfasts, and settled into a routine that worked for us. We were living in my house since I had a guest room that we'd turned into a nursery, and an office we could put a daybed in to make a guest room. Jen had been renting, so it was an easy move, and things fit.

For all our fighting, things worked now.

I wasn't going to look fate directly in the eyes and question it.

We made our way to work, driving together because Jen didn't feel like squeezing behind the wheel, and as we walked in, Daisy looked up and smiled.

"There's my favorite pregnant person."

"Aren't your cousins pregnant, too?"

"Yes, but you're my favorite pregnant person in this room. How's that?" she asked as she held out her hand. "May I?"

"Stop asking. You know you're always allowed to."

Daisy laughed. "True, but I don't want to get kicked by *you* and not just the baby."

Jen rolled her eyes as I held back a laugh, going to my desk.

"I only kicked Kane once. And that's because he surprised me."

"I feel like I still have a bruise on my shin," Kane said from the back room. I laughed, settling into this new whirlwind of a life of ours.

Everything was just so happy. We still worked with some dangerous elements, but not always. Now, we fit together and were making it work. I didn't know what was in store for us for the future, but there were no maybes about who we were now.

And didn't that make me sound like a greeting card?

I didn't care, though. Because my wife was gorgeous, pregnant, happy, and could still kick my ass.

What more could a man want?

"So, are you off this next week?" Jen asked, and Daisy nodded. "I have a friend's wedding."

"Someone not related to you?" I asked, incredulous.

"I know it's shocking to be at a wedding that's not for a Montgomery, like yours was, but yes. It's no one you guys know."

"Interesting," Jennifer drawled, and Daisy rolled her eyes.

"Not that kind of interesting. Have fun while I'm gone. Don't burn the place down."

"I'm not making any promises," Kane put in.

Daisy sighed. I looked over at the desk next to mine and smiled at my wife.

"You doing good?"

"Always."

"The happiness in this room is making me ill," Kane grumbled as he went back to the workroom.

I chuckled as I returned to my paperwork since I had a meeting soon, and Jen had a consult.

This was only our beginning. It may have started with an actual explosion, but I would take the fire, heat, and our version of the unknown every day.

Because I had fallen for my partner, my best friend. And I hadn't realized it until it was almost too late.

I would never take her or our life for granted.

Even when she kicked my butt to remind me.

* * * *

Also from 1001 Dark Nights and Carrie Ann Ryan, discover Happily Ever Never, Nothing but Ink, Captured in Ink, Taken With You, Ashes to Ink, Inked Nights, Hidden Ink, Adoring Ink, and Wicked Wolf.

Sign up for the 1001 Dark Nights Newsletter
and be entered to win a Tiffany Key necklace.

There's a contest every month!

Go to www.1001DarkNights.com to subscribe.

**As a bonus, all subscribers can download
FIVE FREE exclusive books!**

Discover 1001 Dark Nights Collection Eleven

DRAGON KISS by Donna Grant
A Dragon Kings Novella

THE WILD CARD by Dylan Allen
A Rivers Wilde Novella

ROCK CHICK REMATCH by Kristen Ashley
A Rock Chick Novella

JUST ONE SUMMER by Carly Phillips
A Dirty Dare Series Novella

HAPPILY EVER MAYBE by Carrie Ann Ryan
A Montgomery Ink Legacy Novella

BLUE MOON by Skye Warren
A Cirque des Moroirs Novella

A VAMPIRE'S MATE by Rebecca Zanetti
A Dark Protectors/Rebels Novella

LOVE HAZARD by Rachel Van Dyken

BRODIE by Aurora Rose Reynolds
An Until Her Novella

THE BODYGUARD AND THE BOMBSHELL by Lexi Blake
A Masters and Mercenaries: New Recruits Novella

THE SUBSTITUTE by Kristen Proby
A Single in Seattle Novella

CRAVED BY YOU by J. Kenner
A Stark Security Novella

GRAVEYARD DOG by Darynda Jones
A Charley Davidson Novella

A CHRISTMAS AUCTION by Audrey Carlan
A Marriage Auction Novella

THE GHOST OF A CHANCE by Heather Graham
A Krewe of Hunters Novella

Also from Blue Box Press:

LEGACY OF TEMPTATION by Larissa Ione
A Demonica Birthright Novel

VISIONS OF FLESH AND BLOOD by Jennifer L. Armentrout and
Ravyn Salvador
A Blood & Ash and Flesh & Fire Compendium

FORGETTING TO REMEMBER by M.J. Rose

TOUCH ME by J. Kenner
A Stark International Novella

BORN OF BLOOD AND ASH by Jennifer L. Armentrout
A Flesh and Fire Novel

MY ROYAL SHOWMANCE by Lexi Blake
A Park Avenue Promise Novel

SAPPHIRE DAWN by Christopher Rice writing as C. Travis Rice
A Sapphire Cove Noveal

LEGACY OF PLEASURE by Larissa Ione
A Demonica Birthright Novel

EMBRACING THE CHANGE by Kristen Ashley
A River Rain Novel

Discover More Carrie Ann Ryan

Happily Ever Never
A Montgomery Ink Legacy Novella

I love falling in love.
Only I'm the worst at it.

My friends call me a serial first dater and I can't blame them.
All I want is a happy ever after, yet all I find are happy ever nevers.

This is my last chance. After this set up with my friend's tattoo artist, I'm done.
No more dating. No more chances.

If I don't fall in love with Leo Johnson, I'll give up on dating.
Even if it shatters my dreams in the process.

* * * *

Nothing but Ink
A Montgomery Ink: Fort Collins Novella

Clay Hollins knows he needs to stay away from Riggs Kennedy. He doesn't have time to fall for the bearded bartender that haunts his dreams and waking fantasies. Not only is he working long hours at his dream job with Montgomery Builders, but he's raising his three cousins and they need him more than he needs a private life.

After one night of giving in, however, neither Riggs nor Clay can walk away.

Only their lives are chaotic with baggage from Riggs' past and Clay's present and taking a chance on each other might be the scariest yet best decision they ever make.

* * * *

Captured in Ink
A Montgomery Ink: Boulder Novella

Julia and Ronin know their relationship is solid. They've been through hell and back, but their love has stayed true through it all. When Ronin's ex, Kincaid, comes back to town, however, the two realize what they might be missing.

Kincaid didn't mean to leave Ronin behind all those years ago. When tragedy struck not once, but twice, bringing with it the heat of horror, he couldn't face the past he'd left behind. Now, he's back and doesn't know how he fits in with the seemingly perfect couple—especially not when their families will apparently stop at nothing to keep them apart.

* * * *

Taken With You
A Fractured Connections Novella

It all started at a wedding. Beckham didn't mean to dance with Meadow. And he really didn't mean to kiss her. But now, she's the only thing on his mind. And when it all comes down to it, she's the only person he can't have.

He'll just have to stay away from her, no matter how hard they're pulled together.

Running away from her friend's wedding isn't the best way to keep the gossip at bay. But falling for the mysterious and gorgeous bartender at her friends' bar will only make it worse. Beckham has his secrets, and she refuses to pry.

Once burned, twice kicked down, and never allowed to get up again. Yet taking a chance with him might be the only choice she has. And the only one she wants.

**For fans of Carrie Ann's Fractured Connections series, Taken With You is book four in that series.

* * * * *

Ashes to Ink
A Montgomery Ink: Colorado Springs Novella

Back in Denver, Abby lost everything she ever loved, except for her daughter, the one memory she has left of the man she loved and lost. Now, she's moved next to the Montgomerys in Colorado Springs, leaving her past behind to start her new life.

One step at a time.

Ryan is the newest tattoo artist at Montgomery Ink Too and knows the others are curious about his secrets. But he's not ready to tell them. Not yet. That is…until he meets Abby.

Abby and Ryan thought they had their own paths, ones that had nothing to do with one another. Then…they took a chance.

On each other.

One night at a time.

* * * *

Inked Nights
A Montgomery Ink Novella

Tattoo artist, Derek Hawkins knows the rules:
  One night a month.
  No last names.
  No promises.

Olivia Madison has her own rules:
  Don't fall in love.
  No commitment.
  Never tell Derek the truth.

When their worlds crash into each other however, Derek and Olivia will have to face what they fought to ignore as well as the connection they tried to forget.

* * * *

Adoring Ink
A Montgomery Ink Novella

Holly Rose fell in love with a Montgomery, but left him when he couldn't love her back. She might have been the one to break the ties and ensure her ex's happy ending, but now Holly's afraid she's missed out on more than a chance at forever. Though she's always been the dependable good girl, she's ready to take a leap of faith and embark on the journey of a lifetime.

Brody Deacon loves ink, women, fast cars, and living life like there's no tomorrow. The thing is, he doesn't know if he *has* a tomorrow at all. When he sees Holly, he's not only intrigued, he also hears the warnings of danger in his head. She's too sweet, too innocent, and way too special for him. But when Holly asks him to help her grab the bull by the horns, he can't help but go all in.

As they explore Holly's bucket list and their own desires, Brody will have to make sure he doesn't fall too hard and too fast. Sometimes, people think happily ever afters don't happen for everyone, and Brody will have to face his demons and tell Holly the truth of what it means to truly live life to the fullest…even when they're both running out of time.

* * * *

Hidden Ink
A Montgomery Ink Novella

The Montgomery Ink series continues with the long-awaited romance between the café owner next door and the tattoo artist who's loved her from afar.

Hailey Monroe knows the world isn't always fair, but she's picked herself up from the ashes once before and if she needs to, she'll do it again. It's been years since she first spotted the tattoo artist with a scowl that made her heart skip a beat, but now she's finally gained the courage to approach him. Only it won't be about what their future could bring, but how to finish healing the scars from her past.

Sloane Gordon lived through the worst kinds of hell yet the temptation next door sends him to another level. He's kept his distance because he knows what kind of man he is versus what kind of man Hailey needs. When she comes to him with a proposition that sends his mind whirling and his soul shattering, he'll do everything in his power to protect the woman he cares for and the secrets he's been forced to keep.

* * * *

Wicked Wolf
A Redwood Pack Novella

The war between the Redwood Pack and the Centrals is one of wolf legend. Gina Eaton lost both of her parents when a member of their Pack betrayed them. Adopted by the Alpha of the Pack as a child, Gina grew up within the royal family to become an enforcer and protector of her den. She's always known fate can be a tricky and deceitful entity, but when she finds the one man that could be her mate, she might throw caution to the wind and follow the path set out for her, rather than forging one of her own.

Quinn Weston's mate walked out on him five years ago, severing their bond in the most brutal fashion. She not only left him a shattered shadow of himself, but their newborn son as well. Now, as the lieutenant of the Talon Pack's Alpha, he puts his whole being into two things: the safety of his Pack and his son.

When the two Alphas put Gina and Quinn together to find a way to ensure their treaties remain strong, fate has a plan of its own. Neither knows what will come of the Pack's alliance, let alone one between the two of them. The past paved their paths in blood and heartache, but it will take the strength of a promise and iron will to find their future.

Happily Ever Never
A Montgomery Ink Legacy Novella
By Carrie Ann Ryan

New York Times bestselling author Carrie Ann Ryan returns to the Montgomery Ink world with a blind date romance between two unlikely strangers.

I love falling in love.

Only I'm the worst at it.

My friends call me a serial first dater and I can't blame them.

All I want is a happy ever after, yet all I find are happy ever nevers.

This is my last chance. After this set up with my friend's tattoo artist, I'm done.

No more dating. No more chances.

If I don't fall in love with Leo Johnson, I'll give up on dating.

Even if it shatters my dreams in the process.

* * * *

My phone buzzed, and I looked down, frowning.

"What is it?" he asked, the moment broken between us—not that there *was* a moment.

"It's Brooke. Apparently, Leif is outside with Luke and wants her opinion on something. She went out the back with Lake and will meet me later at that boutique Leif's mom owns, Eden."

"Oh. So, they just left you alone with me? Not nice."

I pressed my lips together, unsure what to say. "Honestly, I'm not even sure they noticed you were here." I winced. "Or maybe they did, and they trust you. Or maybe I'm an adult and should just shut up now."

He shook his head and paid for everything, whistling under his breath at the total.

"Being a good uncle adds up."

"Tell me about it. I'm about to have six nieces and nephews."

"I can't even imagine. But I saw how you are with them. They like you."

"Thanks. I like me, too." He winked and grabbed his bags. After I paid for my purchase, I suddenly found myself standing with him outside the bookstore. Alone. This wasn't what I had expected this afternoon.

What was I supposed to do now?

He swallowed hard. "Anyway. I'm going to do something right now. And it's probably a mistake. So don't hit me, okay? Or, you can hit me."

I blinked up at him, confused, and then he set down his bags and pushed my hair back from my face.

I looked up at him, my heart racing. When his lips pressed to mine, I could barely breathe.

It was a slow and gentle exploration, a meeting of lips, barely a taste. An introduction. And then, before I could even figure out what was happening or contemplate his taste, his touch, his need, he pulled away and cursed under his breath.

I blinked, stilling at the sudden tension between us.

"What? What just happened?"

He froze, his eyes wide. "I'm so fucking sorry."

I blinked. "Why are you sorry?" A thread of fear began to weave within me, but I told myself I was mistaken. He had been the one who kissed me. I hadn't pursued him. I wasn't making a mistake again, was I?

"I said I wouldn't kiss you."

I let out a hollow laugh, confused. "Oh. Who did you tell you wouldn't kiss me? No, maybe I don't need to know. You didn't want to kiss me, and you did? Okay."

With my bag in my hand, I turned, confused and not in the mood to figure out exactly what he'd meant by what he said. He wouldn't kiss me but was forced to? What exactly had I done to make that happen?

"That's not what I meant," he said from behind me. I turned, confused and hurt. Wondering why I kept being so awkward. Because this would ruin everything. I didn't want to ruin everything.

"It's okay…whatever you meant. Whatever, Leo. Because I know my worth. It just seems like nobody else does."

And then I left. I texted the girls that I would meet them later and that I wasn't feeling well.

It wasn't a lie because I *wasn't* feeling well. I wasn't feeling much of anything.

And that was it. No more sparks. No more wondering. No more first dates.

Never again.

I was done.

I would do my best not to make myself a liar. And figure out exactly what I'd meant by my worth.

About Carrie Ann Ryan

Carrie Ann Ryan is the *New York Times* and USA Today bestselling author of contemporary, paranormal, and young adult romance. Her works include the Montgomery Ink, Talon Pack, Promise Me, and Elements of Five series, which have sold millions of books worldwide. She's the winner of a RT Book of the Year and a Prism Award in her genres. She started writing while in graduate school for her advanced degree in chemistry and hasn't stopped since. Carrie Ann has written over one hundred novels and novellas with more in the works. When she's not losing herself in her emotional and action-packed worlds, she's reading as much as she can while wrangling her clowder of cats who have more followers than she does.

www.CarrieAnnRyan.com

On Behalf of 1001 Dark Nights,
Liz Berry, M.J. Rose, and Jillian Stein would like to thank ~

Steve Berry
Doug Scofield
Benjamin Stein
Kim Guidroz
Chelle Olson
Tanaka Kangara
Asha Hossain
Chris Graham
Jessica Saunders
Stacey Tardif
Dylan Stockton
Kate Boggs
Richard Blake
and Simon Lipskar